Praise for Denzil Meyrick:

'The poetic dialogue is brilliantly rendered and the characters are reminiscent of those of Compton Mackenzie or Neil Munro . . . sings with the evocation of time, place and people, and the humour and truth behind fishermen's tall tales'
The Scotsman on *A Large Measure of Snow*

'A perfect stocking filler'
LoveReading on *A Large Measure of Snow*

'Absorbing . . . no run-of-the-mill tartan noir'
The Times

'Spellbinding . . . one of the UK's most loved crime writers'
Sunday Post

'Universal truths . . . an unbuttoned sense of humour . . . engaging and eventful'
Wall Street Journal

'Satisfyingly twisted plot'
Publishers Weekly

'Touches of dark humour, multi-layered and compelling'
Daily Record

'Striking characters and shifting plots vibrate with energy'
Library Journal

A note on the author

Denzil Meyrick was born in Glasgow and brought up in Campbeltown. After studying politics, he pursued a varied career including time spent as a police officer, freelance journalist and director of several companies in the leisure, engineering and marketing sectors. Denzil lives on Loch Lomond side with his wife, Fiona.

Also by Denzil Meyrick

D.C.I. Daley thriller series
Whisky from Small Glasses
The Last Witness
Dark Suits and Sad Songs
The Rat Stone Serenade
Well of the Winds
The Relentless Tide
A Breath on Dying Embers
Jeremiah's Bell
For Any Other Truth

Tales from Kinloch
A Large Measure of Snow

Short stories
One Last Dram Before Midnight

Terms of Restitution

A TOAST TO THE OLD STONES

A TALE FROM KINLOCH

Denzil Meyrick

First published in Great Britain in 2021 by Polygon, an imprint of Birlinn Ltd.

Birlinn Ltd
West Newington House
10 Newington Road
Edinburgh
EH9 1QS

www.polygonbooks.co.uk

1

ISBN 978 1 84697 594 3
eBook ISBN 978 1 78885 472 6

British Library Cataloguing-in-Publication Data

A catalogue record for this book is available on request from the British Library.

Typeset by 3btype.com

Printed and bound by CPI Group (UK) Ltd, Croydon CR0 4YY

For my old pal Davie Robertson

He's danc'd awa, he's danc'd awa,
He's danc'd awa wi' the Exciseman.

Robert Burns

PROLOGUE

There are places all over the world that elicit strange feelings of ancient things on the edge of consciousness. Lofty cathedrals, holy spaces and sacred isles possess an ambience of mystery and otherness which pervades the very air.

But the modern world has almost obliterated this otherworldly sense. Gadgets guide the way where once the stars, the sun and signs in nature did the job. Instead of sniffing the air, staring at the sky or observing the behaviour of the creatures who live all around us, radio weather forecasters do the job, announcing with calm, efficient authority that it will be showery – as if this is to be taken as unimpeachable fact by all those who listen through the crackle of static. Even though its veracity may be questionable.

Such is the vanity that has developed within our species, the very idea of knowing without proof, believing without seeing and feeling without touch has become the preserve of the 'mad' or 'unbalanced'. These arcane skills that marked out humanity for millennia have been all but lost.

Yet, when in the dark of night old rafters creek like the rigging of square-rigged schooners, or a barely perceived movement at the corner of the eye – just out of sight – grips a chilled heart, or the call of creatures of the night keeps us from sleep, we are touching the part of our minds that was once as unremarkable as a child's adoration or the embrace of a loved one. None of us can explain a tug on the heartstrings, yet our race could never exist without love, for which there is no rhyme or reason. There is still to be discovered a white-coated scientist who can explain why Joan makes John feel as though he's walking on air; it's just accepted as fact, and that's that.

Deep within every man, woman and child lurks the ability to experience much more than can ever be explained.

How many times do we think of someone then turn a corner only to find them striding towards us? How often does the sinking feeling in the pit of the stomach presage the very worst events in our lives?

Trust it or reject it, there exists the ability to see and feel beyond ourselves, our realm, our mundane reality. It harries the primal part of our minds, as it has done since our time began. Especially when we find ourselves in a place where past and present meet, where time, it seems, stands still.

On the fertile east coast of Kintyre such a place exists.

On a small rise in splendid isolation stand two stones. One is rough and squat, less than the span of three hands in height, the other, slightly taller, is slender and smooth to the touch.

When first encountered, these stones can easily be mistaken for random outcrops of gneiss deposited by the tumults that have shaped our Earth for billions of years. There is little remarkable about them, apart from their resemblance to a short, fat man standing beside a tall, elegant woman.

But take a closer look, and something else may touch your soul. At the top of the smaller rock there is a dip, almost like a bowl. Within, lie the red-rusted remnants of old pins left by farmers in recent centuries. For this has long been a place where 'votive offerings', as archaeologists call them, were deposited. On the other stone, there are marks, writing perhaps – almost weathered away – but not in any hand we now recognise.

But the stones – 'The Couple', the Vikings called them – are now hard to find. Yes, they still stand on the little rise that once afforded them views across the sound. But the only sight they now enjoy is that of tightly spaced fir trees that encase them in a dark forest where neither beast nor man stirs; from where sunlight is banished by the intertwined canopies of pine needles. They exist in silence, with neither tribute nor adoration – well, much of the time, that is.

The time passed a long, long time ago when those who erected these little stones lived. With them they took their meaning. But others, unburdened by the certainties of this age, felt their power.

Over thousands of years, no one has passed by without paying their respects. This, for no other reason than they felt the need to acknowledge the stirring of their souls, for it was known that the Auld Man and Woman, as they came to be known in the modern day, could usher in a fine harvest, bring back the deer that life so depended on in their crude settlements, or some good fortune that everyone still requires.

No sleek dragon boat passed by without leaving a memento of its visit, by way of gold or an engraved ship's name or that of a leader. The weather has worn down these messages, heartfelt offerings of those who came before us, and upon whose shoulders we stand. They are now little more than shadows.

But while trees can last an age, stones are eternal, even when forgotten. And as the tall pines grew all around them, soon came the day when men cut down the wood. Once more the stones stared across the slow waters of the sound and felt the heat of the sun.

And there they remain – and always will, no matter how many new trees grow. For they have the power of the Thin Places.

Kinloch, July 1912

The sky above the small town was deep, deep blue, a hue that only the most glorious of summers could conjure up. The loch glinted like a sea of precious stones, and the big houses on the hill shimmered in the haze. Heading for the remains of the old fort, a gull flapped lazily in the air, its screech echoing across the bay.

And it had been a good summer for fishing, too. Kinloch's fleet of little ring-net boats had chased plentiful shoals of herring and mackerel until their nets all but burst. Fishermen were in funds, and consequently so was every other business in the place, whether they be butchers, bakers or even candlestick makers. Though it had to be said that Tam Douglas, proprietor of the hostelry that bore his name, smiled broader than most.

When the fishing was good and the sun shone, Kinloch was one of the best places in the world. Only in the long dark winter, or a bad season, were pennies counted; then, anxious shopkeepers looked up and down the windswept streets for their next customer, and the menfolk would gaze out at a sea seemingly bereft of marine life. Meanwhile, always at the very heart of family life, women worked harder than ever to make do the best they could to feed their children.

But today, these times seemed like a distant memory.

The boy watched as his father's nimble hands worked at the net, the bodkin flashing in the bright sunlight with every turn of his fist. He marvelled at the dexterity; how his father could take in the activity around the harbour, have conversations as he puffed on the pipe clamped in his mouth, and repair the net, all at the same time. It was as though his hands were possessed of their own will, the product of many years' practice.

Alastair Hoynes decided to take a break. He got to his feet, stretched and yawned. The crew of the *Red Dawn* were busy resetting a mast, while Archie Robertson – never the most industrious fisherman – lay aboard the *Raven* on a pile of nets soaking up the heat, his flat cap pulled down over his eyes. On the road between the twin piers, ranks of barrels stood to attention, waiting for the women to pack them with fish and salt. Hands red raw, hair pushed under scarfs or pinned back in neat buns, their songs and chatter drifted across the harbour.

The boy cocked his head, keen to make out a song or a scatter of words. 'I canna make out the tune, Faither.'

Alastair inclined his head. 'No, nor me, son. I think it's fair tae say that there are few Mod gold medals to be found amongst that lot. Och, but it keeps them happy at their toil, so there's no harm in it at all, Sandy.'

The boy with hair turned golden blond by the salt sea and summer sun nodded sagely. 'Mother says they're all torn-faced auld scunners.'

His father eyed him keenly. 'Your mother has a habit o' finding scunners where none are to be had. I'm sure she was only speaking in jest.'

'She said you were a miserable bugger on Saturday night when she was at her purse.'

Alastair nodded. 'Aye, I daresay. But her bark is worse than her bite. And you shouldna be telling tales behind her back – she's the only mother you'll ever have, and you'll miss her when she's gone. I miss mine to this very day, and she died afore the century turned, God bless her.'

Sandy felt ashamed. His father's rebuke was mild, but he wished he hadn't opened his mouth. While his mother's admonishments were as sharp as the carpet beater with which she caught him on the back of his legs by way of punishment, his father was a more subtle disciplinarian. Sandy had never heard him raise his voice, much less engage in the idle gossip that seemed to be the pastime of just about everyone else he knew – including his mother. He studied the man, imagining himself standing tall, a lick of grey at the temples of his otherwise golden hair, face tanned under the heat of many summers accentuating his bright blue eyes.

'What are you staring at?' Alastair regarded his son over the briar pipe as he tamped in more tobacco.

'Why do we have such blond hair, Faither?'

Alastair puffed his pipe back into life. 'Now, you've fair hit upon an interesting question there, Sandy.'

'How so?'

'My auld grandfaither told a tale about the men fae the north.'

'Glasgow?'

'No, son, much further north than that. At least, that's from where they hailed originally.'

Sandy puzzled upon this for a moment or two, closing one eye against the sun's reflection on the clear water of the loch. 'I'm no' getting you at all.' He stared back up at his father.

'Do they teach you nothing at thon school?'

'Aye, but it's all that arithmetic and English. Mrs Henderson says if you've no' got your letters and numbers you might as well stick your heid in a pail and walk aboot wearing it for the rest o' your days.'

'And she has the right o' it, too. You'll no' go far if you canna tally up the fish you've caught or write a note or two, and that's a fact. But is that all they teach you?'

'How tae sit up straight and the like. But other than that it's reading and counting all day long.' Sandy sighed at the thought of returning to school in a few short weeks.

'Did she never tell you o' the Vikings?'

'No, no' a word. Maybe that's for next year.'

'Well, I'll give you a head start. Here, take a seat on these nets and I'll enlighten you.'

The boy listened to his father intently as he told tales of the men from the north. They were a frightening bunch, that was for sure. He fretted at the stories for a moment, picturing the dragon boats of which his father spoke sailing into the loch and putting men to the sword and ravishing the women. But when he found out how they'd settled the land and made it their own, and what fine fishermen and boat builders they were, Sandy became more amicably disposed towards the Vikings.

Instinctively, like the schoolboy he was, he held up his hand to ask a question.

'Aye, what dae you want to know?'

'What's "ravishing", Faither?'

Alastair cleared his throat, took a long draw of his pipe and stared out to sea. 'Och, it's too hard to explain everything right now. But you'll learn aboot it in time, I'm quite sure.'

'Do you ravish Mother every noo and then?'

Alastair raised an eyebrow. 'Nah, son. If there's any ravishing tae be done in oor hoose, it's your mother that does it. But don't worry aboot that aspect just this minute. There's mair to this tale.'

Sandy detected a flush of red under his father's tanned cheeks but put the whole thing down to the heat of the day. 'So they came and made us all slaves, or the like?'

'Aye, there was slavery that went on, that's for sure. A damnable thing that they canna be very proud o' if they look back on it now.'

'Where are they now?'

Alastair took to his feet again and stood tall, raising his head proudly like some of the heroes Sandy read about in his comic books. He had a distant look in his blue eyes. 'You're looking at one right this very minute.'

Sandy was confused. He keeked past his father, fearful that he was missing something. Or that, in the worst case, he had a squint like poor wee Donnie MacKay and his father had assumed he was looking at something else entirely.

'No, it's me, you dolt – aye, and you!'

'Eh?'

'We're off the Vikings. That's where oor blond hair comes fae. Remember, they were fine seafarers, and so are we. It's been passed down through the generations. In the blood, if you like.'

'So they were a thirsty lot too, then?'

'Why do you say that, son?'

'Because mother says you've got a fair drouth.'

'What did I tell you about telling tales?'

'Sorry.' Sandy's mind was a tumble of ideas. He couldn't picture himself cutting anyone down with an axe or a sword

8

– far less his father or grandfather being about such wicked business. Perhaps their side of the family had been part of a much less bloodthirsty lot.

'I have a book in the house. I'll let you read it if you help me get these nets back aboard.'

So, under the bright summer sun of the late afternoon, father and son readied their neat little boat for dawn the next day, and another trip out to catch the fruits of the sea.

For young Sandy, however, he would never think of himself again the same way. He was from the cold north, where men wore helmets adorned with bull horns and pleated their long fair locks and beards before jumping into boats, all set for a day of fighting and ravishing – whatever that was. He resolved to ask Ranald Kelly the next day, if he could. Ranald, being a bit older than Sandy, was a fount of knowledge. If anyone knew about ravishing, it would be him.

As they stepped back onto the pier, Alastair took his son by the hand and turned him to face Kinloch's fleet of fishing boats, sitting in the crowded harbour like the herrings being packed into barrels of salt on the pier opposite. 'Take a look at the line of the craft – their shape, Sandy.'

The boy cast his eye proudly over *Maggie*, his father's vessel. 'Aye, right bonnie, Faither.'

'Aye, bonnie they are, son. But like us they have their roots wae the Vikings. Sure, they're only dragon boats cut down to size a wee bit. I tell you, Sandy, when we're back out to sea tomorrow, just close your eyes and you'll feel your ancestors in your bones. There's a place up near Firdale where they had their great hall. Aye, they'd head there on a cold night for feasts and a good few tankards o' ale. I'll show you where it is, though there's no' much to see now, apart fae the stones.'

Together they walked back up the pier. Secretly, Sandy was pleased that the Vikings enjoyed their tankards of ale. It meant they must have had a drouth, right enough. So, his mother wasn't always wrong.

1

Kinloch, January 1968

The paralysing snows at the end of the old year had given way to miserable, wet and windy weather. Engorged burns frothed down the hills and glens, turning the loch a peaty brown. Mrs Longmuir's dress shop experienced a flash flood, her latest batch of miniskirts ruined in the process. A gaggle of young women, who had waited for weeks to purchase the latest fashion from Carnaby Street, turned on their high heels and, disappointed, tripped back home with nothing new to wear.

Hogmanay had been a miserable affair. Only the hardiest revellers scuttled from house to house clutching bottles, lumps of coal and black buns. For old habits died hard in Kinloch. Tradition here held fast, where it had fallen away in many other parts of Scotland. Those with red hair stood forlornly in doorways until a suitably tall and dark individual arrived to be First Foot, thereby affording much needed shelter from the elements for all concerned.

This tradition went back to the days when to find anyone without the dark hair and the sallow skin of the area's original inhabitants on the threshold of one's home was to stare death in the face. But Picts, Celts and Norsemen had long mingled to live in relative peace and contentment in Kinloch, the wrongdoing of the ages forgotten.

Sandy Hoynes glowered through the wheelhouse at the rain that was beating like a thousand tiny drums on the *Girl Maggie*. With both he and Hamish in such an enclosed space, each puffing away at their pipes, the atmosphere was, to say the least, thick.

'Man, the third of January. A mair miserable day in the year canna be found,' declared Hoynes.

'Aye, Hogmanay seems like a lifetime ago, and it's only a couple o' nights back,' agreed Hamish.

Hoynes turned a leary eye on his first mate. 'You fairly made the most of it, right enough. Fair puggled you were, like auld Jock Mackenzie at the head o' the pipe band wae a half-bottle sticking oot his jacket pocket. Drunk as a skunk, you were. And let me tell you, if you have any ambitions as a singer, you can just forget them. You fair murdered "My Granny's Heilan' Hame" in oor hoose. Peeny tells me you were shouting aboot free love by the time you made it to his place.'

'It was "All You Need Is Love". The Beatles sang it in front o' the whole world last year.'

'That's as maybe. But if you've any ambition to turn yourself into one o' these hippies, just rein it in. For a start, you haven't got the hair for it, and you'll have to find another berth. There's been enough calamity on this vessel wae narcotics without you embracing them on a permanent basis.' Hoynes drew deeply on his pipe and remembered his fevered lobster dreams while under the influence of a mistakenly administered hallucinogenic. He shivered. 'From now on, the only intoxicant that will be tolerated on this vessel is good old-fashioned whisky.'

Hamish ran his hand through his thinning hair. The fact that his skipper could always find a way of bringing his encroaching baldness into the conversation was a regular irritant. In any case, from what he could remember, Hoynes's accusations were wildly exaggerated. Yes, he'd enjoyed the New Year celebrations to the full, but so had his various hosts; this meant that he wasn't in the slightest ashamed. The dark days of midwinter were brightened up by Hogmanay, and that was a fact – it was the whole point of the thing. With the notion of Christmas still a relatively new concept in the West of Scotland, the old ways still held sway.

Hoynes cleared his throat, frequently a precursor to a portentous statement. 'I have something to tell you, Hamish.'

'A cold hand grabbed Hamish's heart. His mother had been in fine fettle when he'd left her early that morning. In any event, he'd been with Hoynes the whole day, so if anything had happened to her, he'd have found out at the same time as his skipper. Mind working overtime, his next thought was as to the future of his employment. 'You're no' retiring, are you?'

'Retiring? Wae my lassie stepping out wae a police sergeant and a wedding in the offing – no' to mention my wife's insatiable appetite for spending money. I'll no' be able to retire until 1999!'

'That's an ambitious statement, skipper. Man, you'll be kicking a hundred by then.'

'When I was a boy there were fishermen working well into their eighties, and that's a fact. Wae all this modern medicine and the like, folk will soon be looking at a hundred years old like we do turning twenty-one these days. I was up at the clinic wae my bunions the other day. You should see the contraptions they have up there now. I wouldn't have been surprised if Frankenstein's monster had come lumbering oot the surgery. Gravediggers must be fair fearing for their jobs.' He nodded his head in self-confirmation of this reasoning.

'So what is it you have to tell me?'

Hoynes stroked his bushy white beard, a further indication of something monumentous. 'You're no boy any more, Hamish. Man, every time I look at your hairline that very thought strikes me.'

Hamish sighed, but thought it better to keep quiet lest whatever it was Hoynes had to say be further delayed.

'You'll be aware of the tradition we fishermen have around this time o' year.'

'Getting drunk and moaning aboot the weather?'

'No such thing! I'm talking aboot our trip to celebrate the Auld New Year. As you know, it's a privilege only afforded to the senior mariners in the fleet. A rare honour it is to be invited, that's for sure.'

Hamish ruminated upon this 'honour'. As far as he was aware, a group of old-timers took off to take in the old New Year on the twelfth of January each year at a tumbledown hut on the east coast of the peninsula. This was in commemoration of the turn of the date before the Gregorian calendar took over from its Julian predecessor. It was a regular habit of certain Kintyre menfolk to take off to various places on the coast in the summer. To facilitate this pastime, old huts had been thrown together from driftwood and anything else that came to hand. There, they would drink and tell tall tales over a weekend, getting back to nature and enjoying male companionship, away from their wives, who, with very few exceptions, ruled every roost.

The fishing community had taken this idea one step further. But a night spent in a dilapidated old hut with equally old men in order to celebrate the old New Year filled Hamish with horror. The word 'old' turned over in his mind. However, he knew that an arcane honour was being bestowed upon him, and as his father had never received the invitation, he realised this turn of events would please his mother greatly.

'I can tell you're thinking,' said Hoynes. 'Your mouth's hanging open like a beached cod.'

'I'm just surprised, that's all. My faither never got to go.'

Hoynes pursed his lips. 'Well, your faither could be right argumentative after a few drams. As you know, he'd more than a passing fondness for the water o' life.'

'Water o' death, in his case.'

'Aye, sad indeed. For when he wasn't in his cups, he was a fine man.'

Hamish nodded meekly at this. There was no doubt that his father's monumental whisky consumption had hastened his premature demise – though many of his maritime colleagues were of the opinion that his drinking was the product of an unhappy marriage, rather than any weakness of character. After all, whisky was like food, a fundamental sustenance. Any overindulgence was surely a reflection of the unfortunate course of one's life, not an addiction. Hamish had never been taken in by this reasoning.

'So, we set off early on the twelfth. You'll note I had to pull plenty strings to get you there. Make sure you don't affront yourself wae any o' this free love business. My reputation is at stake here, and you know how much store I place on that.'

Hamish nodded in solemn agreement. Many occasions where his skipper's reputation had been brought into question paraded themselves before his mind's eye. But, all in all, it was nice to be appreciated by his more senior peers, and by his reckoning, he'd be by far the youngest present.

'I'll be there, skipper. And thank you.'

'Och, your mother will likely cook up a storm tonight in celebration. A nice stew, I'm thinking.'

'It's fish pie tonight.'

'And a more nourishing dish you canna consume.' Satisfied that he'd done his good deed for the day, Hoynes tamped some more baccy into his pipe and puffed vigorously, a look of great contentment spreading across his face.

Hamish looked out the wheelhouse window as curtains of rain swept across the harbour and dearly hoped that the weather would improve in the next few days.

2

Hamish and his mother were in the kitchen of the Glebe Fields flat they shared – though the elder of the two always referred to it as the scullery. An old black range sat at one end of the room beside a deep Belfast sink. A pitted oak table dominated the space. It was around this very piece of furniture that many of the momentous events in the lives of Hamish's family and their antecedents had been discussed. At this moment, Hamish sat at the head of the table in the chair his father had once occupied.

As always, his mother had excelled herself with the fish pie. But while it was one of Hamish's favourite dishes, he longed to see a plump roast chicken, or a succulent joint of beef. However, Kinloch's fishing community looked after its own. Widows of lost fishermen and their families benefited from a generous supply of free fish. While it was a touching gesture, the tradition did lead to a somewhat limited menu.

'Get that down you,' said his mother. 'In weather like this a man needs as much nourishment as he can get.' She stood over Hamish, hands crossed over her blue apron, making sure he left a clean plate. 'You'll be for a second helping?'

'Aye, that would be grand, Mother.'

'Well, you canna have it.'

'Why not? You just offered.'

'You know I'm not long for this world, Hamish. Goodness knows how few years we've left together before you have to lower me into to the ground down at Kilgreggan.'

'No' again,' muttered Hamish.

'Don't mumble. It's right bad manners. Your faither was a terrible man for the mumbling.'

'Och, he was likely just thinking aloud.'

'No, he was likely just drunk. But, whatever his reasons, I don't want you slipping into the habit.' She leaned over her son and removed his plate from the table.

'So, no second helpings, then?'

'As I say, I could drop deid at any time – I'm of the age. You need to snare a wife to look after you in my place.'

'You're only fifty-eight, Mother.' Hamish shook his head at this regular prophesy of imminent demise.

'It's no' just that, son. Being a woman myself, I'm more than well aware of what the fairer sex looks for in a potential husband.'

'Oh aye?'

'It's a fact. And one thing I can tell you for certain sure is that the combination of a receding hairline coupled wae a burgeoning belly isn't something likely to turn a girl's head. The reverse, in fact – more likely to turn her stomach.'

'There's barely a picking on me!' Hamish was indignant.

'Aye, but once you're by thirty the least morsel can add the weight. So, no more fish pie for you this night. You can chew on a carrot if you feel peckish.'

Hamish looked on forlornly as his mother brandished said carrot in front of him, for all the world like Boudicca with her sword. 'I'm actually quite full anyway.'

'That's the spirit, son.'

'I've got some good news.' Hamish had decided to keep his invitation to the Auld New Year celebrations until after dinner.

'Is it a lassie?' She adopted a stern expression. 'Mind, as keen as I am to see you settled and happy wae a nice girl who'll meet all your requirements, you canna hitch your wagon tae the first pony that trots by.'

'Requirements?'

'You know fine what I mean. A man needs more than just a plateful o' fish pie. I'll no' go into details. You canna just spread your seed wae careless abandon.'

'Mother, we've been through this! I value your opinion, but when I meet a lassie I want to wed, it'll be my own choice. We're no' going to wade through the last six generations of her family and look for phantom murderers, smugglers or sneak thieves, like we did the last time.'

'Sandy Hoynes was talking nonsense. That lassie was off a bad lot, no doubt about it. If you'd any sense, you'd have realised yourself just by the look o' her.'

Hamish brushed this notion aside with a dismissive wave of his hand. 'Can you sit down, Mother, please. I've something important to tell you.'

'She's in the family way! Some vixen has lured you wae the turn of her ankle – I knew it. Your father had a weakness for that kind o' thing. As well as the drink, obviously.'

'I'm unlikely to be lured by an ankle, Mother. Anyway, it has nothing to dae with women.'

Hamish's mother stared blankly at him for a few moments. She held her head in her hands and sighed loudly.

'Whatever is the matter wae you now?'

'I know that it's all the rage now. I was reading the paper

the other day. But tell me at least that it's no' Sandy Hoynes.'

Hamish was puzzled. 'Is what no' Sandy Hoynes?'

'I realise we live in a different world. And I know what you were trumpeting when you were steaming drunk the other night – all aboot this free love and other such horrors.'

'I was singing a Beatles song.'

'Oh aye?'

'Yes! Och, you're just as bad as the skipper.'

'You'll no' be able to stay in Kinloch. These tendencies might be tolerated where they Beatles come fae, but the folk here won't look at you favourably if you're stepping oot wae another man – especially one near auld enough to be your grandfaither.'

'Heavens, how have we got to this? The working o' your mind's a mystery to me, Mother.'

Drying her eyes with the hem of her apron, Hamish's mother regarded him warily. 'So you're no' that way inclined?'

'No, I'm not. And even if I was, Sandy Hoynes wouldn't be the object of my affections.'

'So, it's plain that you've thought about it.'

'Honestly, Mother! All the dreadful things going on in the world and you perplex yourself with issues that are private between folk. You need to find some kind o' interest to keep your mind occupied.'

'I beg your pardon! It's a full-time job making sure you're fed, watered and have clean clothes to put on your back. Do you think this hoose runs itself? I'm telling you, don't expect Sandy Hoynes to run after you the way I do. You'll be pressed into service domestically in that relationship, make no mistake.'

'I'm no' *taking up* with Sandy, Mother. I've been invited to the Auld New Year celebrations. You know, up near Firdale.'

The expression on his mother's face transformed. Then she looked suspiciously at her son. 'You're just pulling my leg.'

'No, Sandy imparted the news to me this very afternoon.'

Her expression was suddenly doubtful. 'Did he . . .'

'Don't you dare! It's got nothing to dae wae that, Mother. It's a grand tradition in the fishing community, as you know. I'm privileged to be asked.'

'Aye, you are that. Your faither never sniffed it. But we all know why that was.'

'Time to put that behind us. Poor faither was his own worst enemy. It's best to let it lie.'

Without taking time to reply, Hamish's mother bustled away from the table.

'Where are you off to now?'

'I'm phoning my friends, Hamish. What do you think I'm doing?' She hesitated for a minute. 'Right enough, I don't need to go to the expense o' phoning them all. Wae Hilda on the exchange the whole o' Kinloch will know in jig time.' She hurried into the hall where the phone resided in splendid isolation on a scalloped table. It was her only indulgence.

Hamish sat back in his chair. He was going to an old hut with some even older fishermen to drink whisky and celebrate the old New Year. Judging by his mother's reaction, you'd think he was taking up a seat in the House of Lords. The young fisherman was convinced he'd never learn the ways of the older generation. These people were an impenetrable mystery to him – especially his mother.

Hearing her excited voice in the hall, he grabbed a spoon, made for the oven and helped himself to a large dollop of fish pie.

3

Being the tenth of January, it was now only two days until the exclusive celebrations of the Auld New Year. Thankfully, the rain had abated. A light grey sky settled over Kinloch as the *Girl Maggie* sailed past the island and towards the harbour. Though a few streetlights were popping into life along the esplanade, given the time of year, there was still a couple of hours of light left in the day. But judging by the flurry of black smoke issuing from the metal chimney that ran up the side of the wheelhouse, and the look on Sandy Hoynes's face, he was in a hurry to reach port.

'You're fair hammering the old girl,' Hamish observed as he took in his skipper's countenance; there was a steely-eyed, pipe-clenched determination he rarely witnessed.

Hoynes nodded grimly. 'All day the day I've been thinking it was the ninth. It's my wife's fault.'

'How so?'

'She has me fair bamboozled wae a new calendar in the kitchen. Aye, plenty o' admirable photographs, but the dates are too small. I'll have to see if Mr Keith at the newsagents has some 1968 ones left, because if we carry on this way I'll be heading for my Christmas dinner a week late. It's called style o'er substance, Hamish. A thing to avoid at all costs. A bit like that revolving door they installed at the King's Hotel last year.'

Hamish thought for a moment. 'I canna say I hold that in any regard. Wae doors generally, there should be no necessity to pause and think before you use them – in my opinion, at least. Man, but that one at the King's Hotel is an article to beware of, and no mistake.'

'As poor Connie MacCallum found to her cost just a fortnight ago.' Hoynes shook his head. 'A fine wedding day fair ruined.'

'What happened?'

'Och, nothing more than a simple case o' mistiming. You know how it is wae thon door. You've got to judge your moment before committing yourself. They tell me poor Jock Tolly was stood out in the pouring rain for near half an hour, feart to put as much as a toe in the thing.'

Hamish nodded in agreement. 'The bugger caught me a right dunt on the knee just after Christmas. Then it had the cheek to fling me into the lobby like a gutted herring. It's only because I battered into big Robbie McQuilkin that I was able to keep my feet.'

'You'd have been carrying a fair cargo o' whisky if your antics at Hogmanay were anything to go by, eh?'

Hamish chose to ignore this barb. 'You've no' told me what happened at the wedding.'

'Oh aye.' Hoynes cleared his throat. 'It being her big day, Connie was dressed up to the nines. A white wedding dress wae one o' they trains.' Hoynes turned to Hamish with a knowing look.

'White?'

'Aye, did you ever? But that means nothing these days. It's all this free love that you're never done wae that's to blame.'

'It was a song!'

'Indeed, just as you say. Anyhow, the bonnie bride gets oot o' the taxi wae the help o' the bridesmaids. Just as pretty as a picture, she was. They'd managed to cover up her acne really well wae a hefty dab o' makeup.'

'The poor lassie's fair afflicted wae the plooks, right enough.'

'In any event, her being all jangled wae the excitement o' the day and all, she made straight for thon revolving door as though she was walking into her own front room.'

'A mistake, no doubt about it!'

'A mistake! She managed to get herself into the wee wedge, right enough. But then the husband pushed his way in beside her. Of course, as you know, there's only room for one body in any part o' that thing.'

'And Tommy Shaw is a big lump o' a lad.'

'He is that. I'd been fair dragged doon to see the bride by my good lady. It never ceases to amaze me how women get themselves so worked up at the sight o' a wedding. It's the same wae babies. One glimpse o' a cot and they're blubbering like a man aboot to be hanged.'

'That's a hellish thing, too.'

'We've seen the last o' that in this country. Don't you worry, when you get up to no good full o' narcotics and free love, the most you'll get is a few years behind bars.'

Hamish chose not to take the bait. 'You're losing the place, Sandy.'

'Aye, just so. So, there's the happy couple crammed into the same compartment of the door. Her face was fair pressed up against the glass. Man, you could see right up her nose. No' a bonnie sight, Hamish. Especially for a lassie on her wedding day. Well, anxious to free him and his new wife,

Tommy gives the door a right shove. But he's never realised his own strength. Before you know it, the bloody thing's away like a merry-go-round at the fair. There they are spinning aboot in the revolving door, feet going like the clappers, fair terrified to make a wrong move in case a limb is lost, or the like.'

'Heavens! That sounds dire, right enough.' Hamish took a comforting draw on his pipe.

'But there's worse to come. You see, all the time they're rotating in the door, her train is wrapping itself round the mechanism in the middle o' the damned thing. Suddenly, without any warning, it comes to a standstill, the pair o' them neither in nor oot.'

'Imagine!'

Hoynes held up a chubby forefinger. 'But in the process o' the door coming to a sudden halt, poor Connie fair rattles her hooter off the glass. Och, there was blood everywhere. She's greeting, all the women are greeting, and big Tommy's looking as though he wished he'd stayed at his mother's hoose and enjoyed a dram or two in front o' the wireless instead o' all this marriage lark.'

'What a shame. Did they carry on with the proceedings?'

'Not at all. It took young Charlie Murray the joiner near an hour to free them. By the time Connie was liberated they'd to rush her up to the cottage hospital wae her nose. Bent as a question mark, it was. Man, has she no' been cutting aboot like a panda for the last couple o' weeks. A finer pair o' black eyes I've yet to see.'

'And what aboot Tommy?'

'He was that shaken they had to help him into the bar.' Hoynes took another puff on his pipe. 'Mind you, they'd to help him back oot four hours later. He had a fair swallow, by all accounts. But who can blame the man? Starts off the day wae thoughts o' the marital bed and ends up getting assaulted by a door and flung oot o' the hospital when he goes to visit his new wife because he's fair steaming. And all of it down to that damned door.'

As Hoynes was relating the sad tale of Connie MacCallum's wedding, they were nearing the harbour. Hamish squinted in the fading light at an unusual vehicle parked at the head of the new quay. The grey Bedford van looked perfectly normal apart from what appeared to be the installation of a small shed where the roof should have been.

'What on earth is that?' said Hamish.

'Ah, good!' Hoynes peered out of the wheelhouse window. 'That's Donnie Robertson fae Wellside distillery.'

'And what's he about, skipper?'

'Knowing fine we were heading up the east road in a couple o' days, he asked me if I could deliver a few cases of whisky – for the laird, you understand. He doesna like taking the van up that way as she's a wee bit top-heavy, and you know the twists and turns involved.'

'You can say that again,' said Hamish. 'But it looks like he's built his hoose on the back there.'

'He's no' much o' a coachbuilder, right enough – no, nor timekeeper neither.'

'How so?'

'He wisna due on the pier until after dark.' Hoynes adopted a demure butter-wouldn't-melt expression. 'Och, we'll maybe just have to sample a dram or two while we wait for sunset. It wouldn't be right to send the Laird o' Firdale inferior whisky, would it?'

Hamish shook his head.

4

By the time the sun had set, Hoynes, Hamish and Donnie had passed the whisky as being suitable for consumption. So, under the scythe of a waning winter moon, with the help of the winch, six cases of the finest Wellside malt whisky were hauled aboard and stowed in the hold under a stout tarpaulin.

Hoynes tied up at the very end of the new quay, an unusual berth for the *Girl Maggie*. Only a curious cat watched them from within a tumble of old nets. The harbour was as quiet as the town itself, for it took the good people of Kinloch a few days to get properly back into the swing of things after the New Year.

Donnie drained the tin mug of whisky and eyed the skipper under his brows. 'Have you decided if you're available for that other wee favour we spoke about?' he said, his bright red hair doing its best to escape from the flat cap that was pushed back on his head and now at a jaunty angle.

Hoynes swirled the remnants of the whisky round in his mug, brows furrowed. 'Aye, well that depends, Donnie. As you know, we're heading up for a celebration that night, plus we'll have guests on board. It would have to be worthwhile to take on such a – well, *delicate* mission under those circumstances.'

Donnie nodded solemnly. 'I reckon such difficulties could be taken into account if you were willing to consider it.'

Hamish looked between the pair, his mind working overtime. He was well aware that his skipper was happy to bend the rules here and there if it meant an extra few bob. However, he got the impression that the deal that was being discussed, though tangentially, was of greater import than anything he'd witnessed in his time as first mate. Hoynes had adopted the expression of a sheriff about to hand down his judgment on some wrongdoer.

'How many cases?' Hoynes asked.

'Maybe thirty,' replied Donnie. 'Mind you, we started out wae thirty-five. But, och, there was some natural wastage and breakages to be considered.'

'To be expected wae such a delicate cargo, right enough.'

Donnie, a tall man, put his arm round Sandy Hoynes's shoulder and led him further down the deck, their conversation now out of Hamish's hearing.

The first mate looked on as Donnie whispered into Hoynes's ear. The old skipper stroked his beard, then muttered something in a low voice. The two men looked out across the loch, still and striped with the bright glimmer of streetlights.

Suddenly, hands were outstretched, and the pair smiled convivially at each other.

'A fine piece o' business, right enough,' Hoynes declared in his normal voice.

'Just perfect,' said Donnie.

Hoynes turned to Hamish. 'Are you up for a wee bit overtime the night? I'll make it worth your while.'

'What's to be done?'

'A deed o' mercy,' said Donnie.

'Aye, Donnie has the right o' it, Hamish. You'll be aware o' the price they're charging for a dram at the Firdale hotel?'

Hamish shook his head.

'Well, all I'll say is that it's in excess o' extortionate. Man, it's like the profiteering experienced during the war. Poor men – aye, and a fair portion o' women – are right thirsting for a small libation, but no' willing to sell their own weans for the privilege. As is only right,' he added through a cloud of pipe smoke.

'It canna be as bad as that, Sandy?'

'Every bit! Auld Jamieson that has the hotel up there is as grasping a man as you'll meet. I wouldn't be surprised at all if he was descended fae the moneylenders at the temple. You'll remember their fate, for I know you're well acquainted wae the Scriptures, a must for any man, never mind a fisherman.'

Hamish mulled this information over. For some reason, injustice made his blood boil. He supposed that this emotion stemmed from the way his father had been dispossessed of the family fishing boat as he descended further into the bottle. But in any event, the thought of the poor people of Firdale being extorted by the wicked hotel proprietor was enough to make up his mind. 'I'm your man, Sandy,' he said, the gleam of the righteous in his eyes.

With the three of them crammed into the cab of the distinctively modified Bedford van, Donnie drove out of the town then took the road to Blaan. There was little in the way of moonlight and only a feeble glow from the headlights, so

Hamish had to squint to make out where they were headed. Nonetheless, Donnie appeared untroubled, the cigarette dangling from his mouth tipped by a long curl of ash that, seemingly defying the laws of gravity, remained in place despite his puffing and the bumpy progress of the vehicle.

Hoynes also appeared undaunted by the chancy driving conditions. He sat contentedly in the middle of the three, busy at his pipe and merrily humming reels and jigs to himself – something to which he was prone after the consumption of a few drams.

'So, what are we about?' asked Hamish.

'We're just collecting a few things from Ballywilline farm.'

Hamish thought for a moment. 'Is that no' in the middle o' nowhere?' While he knew most of the farms in the area by name, he was hazy as to their actual whereabouts.

'Och, nothing more than a wee jaunt up a few farm tracks and we'll be there in a jiffy,' said Hoynes.

This information proved to be less than accurate, as they left the main road and seemed to spend an eternity rattling along narrow, rutted lanes that Hamish hadn't known existed. Mercifully, just as he was beginning to regret the whisky he'd consumed and the cheese sandwich he'd had for lunch, they came to a halt at a farm. A solitary light shone from the farmhouse window. The lowing of cattle emanated from an outbuilding.

'I don't know how farmers can live wae the smell,' said Hamish as he alighted from the van into the cool night air.

'They think the very same o' us and the odour o' fish, Hamish. It's a case o' each to their ain. I'm sure if you lived on a dung heap for long enough it would smell as sweet as one o' they French perfumes.'

A thin, sharp-featured man appeared in the farmyard, his way illuminated by a flickering oil lamp. 'Is that you, Donnie?' he said in a loud whisper.

'Who else were you expecting in a van o' this manufacture, Jock?' said Hoynes.

'And no need to ask who you are, Sandy Hoynes, and no mistake! Well, there's a thing. I canna remember the last time I set eyes on you, and us living barely ten miles apart.'

'It's a long time since oor schooldays, Jock.'

'That's for certain sure. Right, we better be about oor business before Jessie is finished her baking. You know fine her opinion o' this lark.'

Jock turned on his heels and headed across the yard towards a shed that loomed before them in the darkness.

5

If it's true what they say about everything being connected, and time working in an infinite, ceaseless wheel, then maybe the events that night, unseen by everyone apart from Gilbert MacIntosh, could have been explained away as fact. But in the cold January darkness of hushing surf and the whispering of branches called into life by a swirling wind, rationale and reason could easily have been distorted into something other.

MacIntosh, a Firdale man by birth and inclination, had spent most of his life as a gamekeeper. Though he'd plied his trade over the course of almost forty years and for a number of masters, he had been happily employed by the Absdale Estate for the last five seasons. His main tasks were to make sure that all was well with the estate's livestock, especially the hens, which produced eggs famous for their taste, quality and size up and down the West Coast.

Tales of persons of ill-intent from Glasgow were hot gossip in the area. Indeed, six of the Semples' best ewes had been wrangled from the farm that skirted Absdale only the previous night. So, fears for the prize hens were at an all-time high.

It is easy to wonder why these precious birds were only contained within their coops in the hours of darkness. But the laird – a free-thinking libertarian – felt strongly that every bird had the right to roam. Indeed, it was posited that this very unusual husbandry was the main reason the end product tasted so good. You didn't need salt on an Absdale egg; with a diet of seaweed they were salty enough. It was said, though not all agreed, that within their creamy, deep yellow yolks, a distinct hint of green could be detected. If eating eggs with a green hue was initially unpalatable to some, once tasted, customers returned again and again to repeat the experience, the consumption of all other eggs foresworn.

However, many other producers in the area disputed this tale. The very idea of hens with a taste for seaweed was, to say the least, daft. But when their profits failed to match those of Absdale Estate, they, too, decided to try a similar method. None had succeeded. Meanwhile, every day without fail, the dutiful Absdale hens, bred to do so over generations, returned to their coops as the sun set. So, as a reward for their faithfulness, their accommodation was guarded as though it contained the most precious of jewels.

Gilbert had been responsible for a wide range of creatures, from pheasants to prize heifers. But when he took on the position of gamekeeper, he was the first to admit that the tutelage of poultry was a novelty. Though, all this time later, here he was, under an overcast sky with only a glimmer of a crescent moon with which to see, making sure that none of his flock came to any harm. With his shotgun broken in the crook of his arm, he was equally ready for fox, fiend or poacher. And though some birds were inevitably lost to predatory creatures during the day, it was his job to guard the hens at night. It was a task he took most seriously.

Gilbert took a long draw on his cigarette: pipes were all very well for those with the time and light to fill them, but his business was done in darkness, so a packet of Woodbines and a box of Swan Vestas were much more convenient.

He sat on a surprisingly comfortable jut of rock studying the dark spread of the Kilbrannan Sound before him, for poachers in this part of the world often went about their clandestine criminality in boats. He could just about make out the loom of the Isle of Arran, but without stars and a full moon, Ailsa Craig and the Ayrshire coast were invisible in the velvet darkness. Even the billions of stars that adorned the heavens were obscured by high cloud. At night, the tang of the sea being subdued, he could smell burning coal from the distant fires of the castle on the other side of the wood beyond the shore. But all was still, with only a gently swirling breeze carrying the smoke from his cigarette to the nor'west.

The first thing he heard over the soothing slip and slide of the tide was the unmistakable sweep of oars as they propelled an unseen vessel forward. Gilbert's heart began to race. It made sense that the men from Glasgow would appear by such means; any kind of engine would instantly attract attention.

Quietly, he edged back into the hedges that bordered the beach, watching, waiting.

The sweep of the oars grew louder, and with it, an unusual feeling of dread filled Gilbert's breast. He'd faced down poachers many times, but something deep inside told him to flee this place, for reasons he could not explain.

But he was a steadfast, conscientious man, and whatever was causing this foreboding, he was determined to carry out his job to the best of his ability.

A shadow of flame appeared on the water. He took a deep breath, ready to move at a moment's notice. But what he saw rooted him to the spot. The fire came from a brazier at the prow of a vessel. It illuminated a large, coiled snake's head and the sweep of a beautifully wrought bow.

Gilbert looked on from the safety of the bushes as the sleek craft passed by only yards from the shore. He could clearly hear voices but couldn't discern what was being said. The words sounded garbled, foreign to his ears. But he stared on, transfixed by the apparition.

He could make out the shapes of men on the craft, all of them in shadow; some were rowing, others stood or lounged in the gunwales.

All bar one.

At the stern of the boat, another brazier flamed in the dark night. A tall man dressed in black stood underneath it, the flickering shadows of flames shining from his leather tunic and breeches. His hair was blond, pulled back in thick pleated knots, his oiled beard long and glistening.

As Gilbert fought to hold his breath, the man turned, looking directly at the bushes where he was hiding.

'A fine night to you!' called the apparition. 'The moon is just right for dark business, yes?' The voice was accented, but plain.

Gilbert fell backwards, gasped for breath, then took off up the short rise and into the trees. His face was slashed and harried by thorn and briar, but he didn't care. His only thought was to escape this vision – this man from another realm, from another time.

6

Hamish rubbed the sweat from his brow under the light of three oil lamps hung about the barn. They had just stowed twenty hay bales into the back of Donnie's van. Well, he and Donnie had done most of the work, while Hoynes and Jock the farmer cackled over old times and cracked even older jokes.

At first, Hamish wondered why on earth they were moving bales of hay until Donnie tripped on the rough earthen floor and a lemonade bottle tumbled onto it. The bottle didn't break; rather it rolled towards Hoynes, who picked it up, a frown on his face.

'Damn me, I might as well have had two o' Jock's coos load the lorry. Hooves would be handier than your slippery mitts.'

Hamish delved into the bale he was carrying. It didn't take long for him to find another lemonade bottle. He unscrewed the cap and inhaled the contents of the bottle. 'I might have known – whisky! Why on earth would you fill old lemonade bottles wae whisky then hide them in hay?'

Hoynes, standing directly under a lamp, shook his head as the blue smoke from his pipe drifted up into the rafters. 'Och, it's plain that you have little understanding of how to carry bottles safely. Man, if they weren't fair encased in the hay, they'd rattle aboot like nobody's business in the back o'

Donnie's van. You know how irregular the road surface is on the way back to the main road.'

Jock's thin face was a mask of concern as he flicked Hoynes an anxious look.

'Now look, you've fair put Jock on edge. It's no' healthy for men o' oor age to be shocked in any fashion. I wouldn't be at all surprised if Jock here went to his bed the night and never woke up again, what wae the trauma o' the whole proceedings.'

Jock looked even more worried. 'Surely you don't think so, Sandy? I keep myself fit, you know.'

'And eat like a sparrow, by the look o' things. You need tae get a bit o' fat aboot you. You'd hardly expect to sell a beef coo in such a pallid, emaciated condition, would you?'

'But nobody's taking me in wae thoughts o' their Sunday lunch, Sandy.'

'These days, wae hippies and the like, you never know just what's in store. The world's fair going off the rails, and that's a fact. Even Hamish is into thon free love now.'

Jock and Donnie gawped at the younger fisherman. But rather than defend this wholly erroneous statement for the umpteenth time, Hamish was inclined to discover more about the contents of the hay bales.

'I'll give you the packaging theory, skipper. But how do you explain the fact that the whisky isn't in whisky bottles?'

'Dae you never read the papers? Sure, there's a glass shortage that would frighten any glazier wae half a brain. Right across Europe, too – something up wae the sand an' all that pollution fae oil tankers you hear aboot on the wireless. It's right wasteful to discard anything when it's perfectly functional. Easy seen you never lived through two World Wars. You'd have taken a dram oot o' a dirty pail, such were the shortages. Am I right, Jock?'

The farmer nodded his head, unconvincingly. 'To be sure, young man. A right hard time it was for one an' all. You couldna even buy a bag o' sweets in Effric's sweet shop in Kinloch. I'd to resort to dunking rhubarb in sugar, just to get the sensation o' a poke o' sweets.'

'Right enough, you've always had a sweet tooth, Jock. You were the same in school. I don't think I ever saw you without a sherbet dab poking oot o' your gob.'

Hamish narrowed his eyes. 'My mother warned me aboot this kind o' caper. She said you were always at some devilment, Sandy.'

'Your mother has a right fertile imagination, so she does. But there's nae harm in her.' Satisfied that he'd offered up a sufficiently feasible explanation as to why lemonade bottles filled with whisky were concealed within hay bales, he cleared his throat. 'Right! Less o' this banter. I'm fair needing my bed. And it must be well past the time you should be oot searching for some o' that free love, Hamish.' He winked at Jock, opened the lemonade bottle and took a swig of its contents before handing it to the farmer. 'My, it's good to note that the whisky has been improved by resting in the hay, Jock. Likely there will be distillers across the country getting up to the same process as soon as they're able.'

'Aye, and their customers will get money back on the bottle when they've finished their dram,' said Hamish with a knowing look.

'Again, you have the right o' it, Hamish. I knew I'd picked the perfect man to be my first mate – despite your hair falling oot wae free abandon. But nobody's perfect. Now, let's get a shift on!'

It took another twenty minutes to stow the van safely with the bales of whisky. Donnie made for the cab with Hamish, as Hoynes wished his old friend goodbye.

Just as they were parting company, though, an apparition in tartan slippers, quilted dressing gown and hair tightly bound up in curlers appeared in the broad doorway of the barn.

'What's all this?' said Jessie as she took in the house on wheels, the two men in the cab and her husband standing beside an instantly familiar figure.

'My, Jessie,' purred Hoynes. 'But you look as good as you did when you were sweet sixteen.' He smiled broadly. 'If it wasn't for the charms o' Jock here, I'd have fair lured you away tae be a fisherman's wife and no' a farmer's, make no mistake.'

'Aye, and I'd have jumped in the loch at the first opportunity to be free o' you. Just what is it you have my poor husband inveigled in?'

'I was just dropping by to say hello, Jessie. Fair missing my auld school chum, right enough.'

'So, you arrived here under the cover of darkness wae a hoose on board a lorry, and this pair o' ruffians just to pass the time o' day wae my husband? You must think I came doon in the last shower, Sandy Hoynes.'

'And a right heavy shower it would have been,' muttered Hoynes under his breath, eliciting a snort of laughter from Jock.

'Well, you've seen him now, you can be on your way. Decent folk should be in their beds by this hour.'

Hoynes produced his pocket watch and squinted at it. 'Man, it's barely seven o'clock. What on earth dae you get up to in bed all that time? It must be a good book you're reading.'

On hearing this, Jock chortled again. But noting that his wife was advancing into the barn, his expression soon changed to one of concern. 'Quick, Sandy, get yourself back in the lorry. She's a fair temper, as well you know!'

For a man of his size and vintage, Sandy Hoynes was remarkably fleet of foot when the occasion demanded. So much so that he covered the distance between Jock and the van with admirable speed, all the time clutching a lemonade bottle of depleted contents. He hoisted himself into the cab. 'Right, Donnie, it's time we were taking oor leave.' As the engine fired into life and the van pulled slowly out of the barn, Hoynes glanced in the wing mirror just in time to see Jessie administer a sharp clip round her husband's ear.

'You're a right man for the flattery, Sandy,' said Hamish.

'In what way?' Hoynes replied, only slightly out of breath.

'Telling the woman she looked as good as she did when she was sixteen. What a plaster you are.'

Hoynes inclined his head towards the wing mirror once more, but Jock and Jessie were out of sight. 'I was speaking nothing but the truth, Hamish. She was never a bonnie lassie and she's just the same to this day.'

Soon, they were rattling their way down the farm track and back to Kinloch, the bottles of whisky safely encased in hay.

7

The morning of the eleventh of January dawned bright, but cold. Had it not been for the gnarled fingers of trees and a brush of frost on the hills, anyone seeing a photograph of the loch and the harbour of bobbing fishing boats would have assumed it was high summer.

A low winter sun shone on a small huddle of men gathered beside the *Girl Maggie* on the pier. They stamped their feet and clapped gloved hands to keep warm, while their frozen breath mixed with the smoke from pipes and cigarettes.

'Just like Sandy to be late,' opined Peeny, his sharp face screwed up in disgruntlement.

Jim McMichael nodded in agreement. 'We should have taken my boat. Man, we'd have been there by now. I hate wallowing in this old tub.'

Malcolm Connelly looked unimpressed by this comment, as he stroked his beard thoughtfully. 'Mind, this auld tub fair beat you out into the loch just a week or two ago.'

'Only because I was distracted when I saw that lassie's heid popping through the hatch like some apparition. I wouldn't be surprised if the boat's fair stowed wae women and ministers. Hoynes likes to chance his luck. And as we all know, that's tempting providence.'

'Aye, I canna say I was convinced by the story o' the gull that was supposed to have guided them back in the snow,' said Donald McKirdy. 'It all sounded a bit far-fetched to me. He's a slippery bugger. Who's to know that he didn't hold up in some wee inlet, watch us all sail by in the blizzard, and wait to return the conquering hero, escaping death by a whisker. He didna take long to get a story out, did he? Everyone had him down wae the best o' us, but he came back wae nothing but the clothes he was standing in – bugger all good to anyone.'

Peeny sniffed his agreement in the cold air.

Andy Duncan, the oldest fisherman present by some margin, smiled broadly. 'You have to admire his brio, mind you.'

'His what?' said Connelly.

'He always comes oot smelling o' roses. He was the same when he was a boy – never got caught, despite all his schemes.'

'The luck o' twenty men, so he has. And he's always at something.' Malcolm Connelly looked sour. 'We all knew Hamish's faither well. The last thing he'd have wanted would have been to see his only son learning every bad habit there is to be had from the likes o' Sandy Hoynes.'

'To be fair, they had little choice. There wasn't a berth to be had in the fleet and they'd lost their own vessel to the money changers at the bank. A damned shame,' said Andy Duncan, the process of age having mellowed his outlook.

'Still, Hamish is working under a right rogue, and no mistake. Only the good Lord knows if we'll make it to the bothy at Absdale. But it was Hoynes's turn, and that's a fact, bad apple or not,' said Peeny.

A cloud of freezing breath rose into the air as the little group murmured in agreement.

'It's a fine day, right enough,' declared Hoynes, appearing as if from nowhere, Hamish at his heel.

'It's yourself, Sandy. Aye, and in good time as always,' said Peeny.

'We were just commenting on how lucky we were to have you at the wheel, what wae the navigational skills you showed getting back through thon blizzard. Man, that was a feat and no mistake. I was reading aboot it in the papers for days. You're a credit to the fleet,' said McKirdy.

'Very kind of you to say so, Donald. At least we have the right weather for our wee jaunt. I expected a right dreich affair, the way it's been the last few days.' Sandy Hoynes looked about with satisfaction at the cold but otherwise benign conditions.

It was Jim McMichael's turn to speak. 'I was just telling the boys how lucky we are to be making passage in the *Girl Maggie*. My boat's built for speed, but you canna beat a vessel broader in the beam for comfort, and that's for sure.'

'And she can get a fair turn o' speed under stern when required. Say, if you were fair rushing oot into the loch, for example.' Hoynes winked at the assembled fishermen, old and young, retired or still on the water.

'Right enough, Sandy, right enough.' McMichael smiled with every part of his face but his eyes, as the rest of the company chortled at the observation.

'Right, let's be aboot it, lads. I don't need to show you how,' said Hoynes.

One by one, the party stepped off the pier and over the side of the *Girl Maggie* across the lapping gap of water as though it was of no consequence. Each man was an experienced fisherman, even young Danny O'May, who at the tender age of twenty-three still had eight years before the mast under his belt, even if he did make Hamish look like a veteran.

It was to this end that Hamish caught the ear of his skipper. 'You never telt me that O'May was part o' all this. I thought I was to be the youngest here – "a rare honour", you said, Sandy.'

'Och, what are you worried aboot? Are you no' just after winning fisherman of the year?'

'Aye, only 'cause he was doon wae the chickenpox.'

'You've no confidence in your own abilities, Hamish. I blame that mother of yours. Fair undermining, she is. But it's my job to make sure that you feel you can take on the world. So, to that end, you'll skipper this fine craft during the entirety of the trip. Young Danny O'May will be your first mate. How does that sound, eh?'

At first, Hamish felt great pride in being trusted – not only with the *Girl Maggie*, but with the responsibility of sailing the most esteemed fishermen in Kinloch to their destination. He also fancied the idea of lording it over young Danny, which made the prospect all the more satisfying.

Hoynes patted him on the shoulder as he passed by. 'I better get oor guests settled. You make ready to put to sea.'

It was only then that something troubling crossed Hamish's mind. 'Does this mean that I've tae stay sober, Sandy? Yous can get fair puggled while I'm at the helm.' He'd reached the conclusion that, along with Danny, his job was to ferry the collected revellers to and from their Auld New Year celebrations. In fact, the invitation was not the honour that his skipper had made it out to be; rather it was a duty to be carried out in strict sobriety. He was a mere functionary, nothing else.

'Man, but you're the most cynical body I know. Of course that's not what I had in mind.'

'Oh, just thought I'd ask,' said Hamish, much relieved.

'Mind you, you'll no' be partaking while sailing there and back, and it wouldn't do to get too tight the night either, just in case the fishery officer is abroad when we're on our way back. Other than that, just you have a good time like the rest of us intend to do.' Hoynes thought for a moment. 'Though, maybe best no' to mention the inclination for thon free love you're so taken wae, eh?'

Hamish didn't bother to argue the point. He knew he could sail back and forth to Absdale in his sleep. And in any case, as his skipper often said, 'The fish guts roll downhill.' So, he would instil a great sense of duty and responsibility into Danny O'May, his junior by seven years, but still more than capable of navigating their way back to Kinloch the next day. In any case, Hoynes and the rest of the more venerable passengers would be in no state to wonder at his level of sobriety. He had the advantage of resilient youth. This thought cheered him as he called for Danny to cast off.

'That's a right pile o' straw you've accumulated aboard, Sandy,' remarked Peeny, examining the deck. 'I hope we're no' sharing quarters wae a coo?'

'Just a wee favour I'm doing. I can guarantee that there's no livestock aboard.' Hoynes glanced around the harbour. There was no sign of the fishery officer or the harbour master. He smiled contentedly as he settled his passengers aboard and Hamish went about the business of setting sail for Absdale.

It was a fine day, right enough.

8

Customs House, Glasgow

Alan Marshall had been surprised by a message left by an anonymous caller. The call had been made prior to his arrival in the office, but his secretary, Blanche Dunlop, had taken the content down verbatim using her formidable shorthand skills.

'Let's go over it again, Blanche,' said Marshall, sitting in his wood-panelled office in Glasgow's India Street. The building's antiquated heating had yet again failed to keep up with the sudden change of weather, and he was glad he'd chosen to wear a pullover beneath his suit to take the chill off the day. As always, the air was thick with tobacco smoke. Marshall sucked on a pen as, once more, he scanned the neatly typed transcript of the call.

'The phone rang, Mr Marshall. I answered in the normal fashion,' said Blanche, her shorthand notebook poised in her hands.

'I think we can take that as read. Let's get into what was said, shall we?'

'Well, just as you see it, sir. I took notes as she was speaking. I think you'll find they're accurate.'

'I don't doubt it, Blanche – no, not for one minute.

I'm more interested in the tone of the call, the person with whom you conversed. What did she sound like?'

Blanche, in her early twenties and already marked out for better things, thought for a moment. Her tongue tipped her front teeth as she went over the conversation in her head. 'She reminded me a bit of my Auntie Amy, I suppose.'

'A Glasgow woman?'

'No, she lives in Ayr – why do you ask?'

'I'm trying to establish her accent, Blanche.'

'I was meaning that she sounded like my Auntie Amy because she was old – maybe in her fifties, or something like that.'

Marshall, who was fifty-two, was yet again reminded how young people perceived age. It was clear that anyone above the age of thirty was considered positively ancient, even though he felt every bit the same as he had in his twenties. Blanche would experience this same cruel deception that life was certain to play, so he decided to say nothing of it. 'Right, a middle-aged woman, then?'

'I'd say old – fifties is old, isn't it? Maybe even a bit older.'

'So, not a young woman. I think we've established that. What about an accent? You mention here that she refused to give any clue as to her own whereabouts but wanted to report happenings in Kinloch, am I right?'

'Yes, though she didn't sound like anyone I know from that neck of the woods, sir.'

'Oh, so you know people from Kinloch?'

'Well, I went to typing school with a lassie from Skye, sir. Kinloch is up that way, isn't it?'

Marshall screwed up his face. He had learned not to be surprised how little the people of Glasgow knew about any part of Scotland beyond the boundaries of their city. He walked over to a large map of Scotland that hung on the wall behind his desk. Pointing to the Isle of Skye then down to the long Kintyre peninsula that jutted out towards Ireland, he addressed Blanche in schoolmasterly tones. 'Actually, it's not up that way at all. While Skye is well to the north of Glasgow, Kinloch is well to the south – do you see?'

'I'd always thought it was up north. Isn't that strange?'

'A common mistake. The people of Kinloch have a distinct tongue – long vowels, odd words and the like. For instance, she might have said "aye" in this fashion.' Marshall's mimicking of the Kinloch accent was accurate. He'd spent two years in the Customs office in the town when he'd first joined up. Though he'd grown to like the place, he was the first to admit that there were few communities like Kinloch – unusual, to say the least.

'Yes, that's it!' exclaimed Blanche, her eyes wide with the intrigue and excitement of it all. 'You are clever, sir.'

Rather pleased with himself, Marshall addressed the rest of the transcript. 'Says here that a vessel called the *Girl Maggie* is involved in the clandestine transportation of illicit spirits – in this case, whisky.' He looked at Blanche levelly. 'Would you say this person was telling the truth? We do get a lot of malicious calls, you know, from people seeking revenge and the like.'

'I'd say she sounded angry, sir – furious, in fact. She mentioned that her husband had been an unwitting party to this, as you can see. I suppose she's just standing up for him.'

'Yes, very interesting,' said Marshall. 'Did you notice anything else during the call – in her tone, I mean?'

'A cow, sir.'

'Now, now, Blanche. There's no need to get personal about this woman. Let's stick to the facts, please.'

'No. What I mean is that I heard a cow, sir. You know that mooing sound they make.' Blanche puffed out her cheeks and executed what could only be described as a reasonably accomplished effort at the imitation of a cow.

Marshall raised his brows and reached for his pipe. 'Very impressive, Blanche. If you find you don't like it here, you can always get a job on the wireless with your impersonations, eh?'

The young secretary was momentarily taken aback. 'Oh no, sir. I don't think I'd like that at all.'

'I was only kidding,' said Marshall as he tamped down the tobacco in his pipe. 'You've been most helpful. I'll take things forward from here.'

Blanche executed what could best be described as cross between a bow and a curtsey before turning on her heels and leaving the office.

Marshall walked to a wall of files set in a metal frame that filled most of one wall in his office. He peered along the rows until he came to 'K' for Kinloch and pulled out a heavy file for further examination.

Sitting behind his ample desk, Marshall flicked through various incidents that had attracted the attention of Her Majesty's Customs and Excise over the years. Most were related to the town's distilleries or the odd individual who had appeared on a vessel looking to flee their home from behind the Iron Curtain and relocate to Great Britain. But these were few and far between, and the majority of cases involving the distilleries amounted to little more than minor pilfering, for which the trader was inevitably punished with a disproportionally high fine.

Having spent half an hour working his way through the

records, he decided to flick to the end of the file, typically where notes of the local collector were appended.

Marshall scanned a few paragraphs of leader prose until he reached the subheading PERSONS OF INTEREST.

He ran his finger down a list until he came to a name strangely familiar from his time in Kinloch: one Alexander Hoynes, skipper of the *Girl Maggie*.

'Well, well, Mr Hoynes, there you are, after all this time,' he whispered to himself as he read a catalogue of crimes and misdemeanours to which the fisherman had seemingly been connected, but without sufficient proof to bring him to book.

Marshall puffed on his pipe and thought back to his two years in Kinloch. The image of a thickset man with fading blond hair and a patchy beard crossed his mind. Yes, he was sure this was the same Sandy Hoynes in which the present senior officer in Kinloch seemed to be so interested.

Marshall reached for the phone on his desk.

9

Though the sail to the destination on the north-east end of the Kintyre peninsula was not a long one, at around the halfway point, conditions in the small cabin below deck were becoming difficult. With every man smoking either pipes or cigarettes, many of the venerable mariners were now coughing and spluttering, their eyes watering.

Even though the whisky bottle was in liberal use, disgruntlement was setting in.

'I'm buggered if I can see the hand in front o' my ain face,' said McKirdy irritably.

'It's like being back in the war,' said Peeny. 'They had me aboard a tug in the Clyde. Man, what a smoky bloody thing it was. But it was like standing on top of a Swiss Alp breathing in sweet fresh air compared wae these hellish conditions. Can you no' do something, Sandy?'

'Och, I had the hatch open a while ago and yous were all complaining it was too cold.'

'You've fair gone up in my estimation,' remarked Andy Duncan, a thin roll-up poking from the corner of his mouth. 'It's many years since I had to endure such an environment at sea. I'm quite sure the galley slaves you hear all about thousands of years ago enjoyed better working conditions than this.

It's a credit to your powers of endurance, Sandy, and no mistake.'

'You'll note there's only one or two o' us in here at any one time under normal circumstances. The human cargo is a great deal larger than I'd normally countenance,' replied Hoynes indignantly.

'I'm just waiting for a lassie to appear fae nowhere,' opined Jim McMichael, engendering a throaty chuckle from the other fishermen.

It was Malcolm Connelly's turn to make a comment. 'Aye, or a Robertson. Man, it must be one o' the few times in all my years there's no' been one o' that clan on this trip.'

'Wee Davie's fair entangled playing wae his banjo. They've a new band on the go – the Vaccineers, would you believe.'

'I heard them at a wedding in November. It's jeest a' wailing and laments. Fair dirges from start to finish,' said McKirdy. 'I was forced to take refuge in the bar downstairs in the County for maist o' the night, their repertoire was leaving me that melancholy. No' a decent reel or jig to be had. Some tale o' a soldier at Culloden and his sweetheart.'

'I was there too, mind.' Peeny thought back to the night in question.

'Aye. She was feart that he'd be killed, so she went in his place.'

'You're right, Donald – cut her hair, the lot. But when she gets back fae the thick o' the battle, she finds him wae another lassie, kilt round his ankles, I don't doubt.'

'Right depressing stuff. He can keep thon banjo, as far as I'm concerned . . . much as I like the man.' McKirdy polished off the last dregs of his whisky. 'I'll have another, if you don't mind, Sandy.'

Hoynes leaned over with the whisky bottle he'd led Hamish to believe was intended for the Laird of Firdale, and poured his demanding guest a bumper. 'You've no heart, that's your problem. There was a tear in my eye when I heard that ballad.'

'Ach, away, man. The only time there's a tear in your eye is when you get a shilling less on a box fae the fish buyer,' said Malcolm Connelly.

Suddenly, Hamish's head appeared though the hatch. 'Skipper, it's thon radio. Fair burst into life just there a minute ago.'

'Did you answer?' said Hoynes.

'No, I got a right fright. By the time I'd recovered, it was too late. You know fine I'm no' acquainted wae the bloody thing yet.'

'This'll be the radio the harbour master forced on you after your meanderings in the blizzards, Sandy?' said Peeny. The rest of the company bowed their heads to disguise their mirth. 'Man, they tell me you and Hamish got that lost in Glasgow when you were buying it, you had to walk into a polis station to ask directions. Country comes tae town, right enough.'

Leaving his mocking companions behind, Hoynes hoisted himself through the hatch to find out what the radio message was all about.

'It's like watching a ewe give birth,' said McKirdy in his wake.

On deck, Hoynes made for the wheelhouse and the 'contraption' – as he'd christened the new radio.

'You're no' covering yoursel' in glory, Hamish.' Hoynes studied the device. He turned a large knob on a panel, grabbed the mouthpiece and spoke loudly and slowly, as was the habit of any man of his nationality and generation when encountering someone from another land. 'The *Girl Maggie* here. Come on, if you would, please.'

'I think you just have to say "come *in*", Sandy,' said Hamish.

'Listen tae you. You took fright as soon as the damn thing came on. Don't lecture me as to its operation.'

'I think it was the harbour master, Mr Hoynes,' said Danny.

'And how do you know that, young man?'

'We've had a radio for years on oor boat. I can get him, if you want?'

'You're a clever lad, right enough. Stand aside, Hamish. It's clear you have none o' the skills necessary for this task. Och, I'm black affronted.'

'We've only had it for three weeks, Sandy. Be fair!'

'You should have picked it up by now.'

'You said no' tae touch it!'

'Have you never heard of initiative? Peer through the window, and fair take in what young Danny's at.'

Reluctantly, Hamish and Danny swapped places, the latter squeezing into the small wheelhouse alongside the ample skipper.

'Right, Mr Hoynes, you just turn this dial to the right number.' Danny did this and picked up the mouthpiece. 'The *Girl Maggie* to Kinloch harbour master, over. Come in, Kinloch harbour master.'

Hoynes looked at Hamish through the murky window. 'See that? Sharp lad this is, right enough. You'll need to watch your back, Hamish.'

Before the first mate could reply, the radio burst into life. Mitchell the harbour master's voice was loud, if somewhat distorted through the round speaker. 'Receiving you, *Girl Maggie*. Go ahead, over.'

Hoynes grabbed the handset from Danny. 'It's Sandy here, you called us, eh?'

There was silence from the speaker.

'You've no' said "over",' said Danny.

'Damn me, whoot a carry on. You don't say "over" when you're on the telephone, so why on here?'

Danny shrugged as Hoynes shouted 'over' as loud as he could into the mouthpiece.

'Sandy, I was just passing on a point o' interest – nothing more, you understand, over.'

'You're a terrible man for the gossip, Mitchell. I didna think that's what this contraption was all aboot . . . *over*.'

Mitchell was silent for a moment. He was an old lobster fisherman himself, and always tried to make sure his former colleagues were as well informed as possible. 'Sandy, I've just had word that the Customs cutter is on her way. She'll be berthed in Kinloch tonight. Just for your information, over.'

What could be seen of Hoynes's face above his beard turned white. 'Here, son,' he said handing the mouthpiece to Danny. 'You tell the harbour master I've a sudden call o' nature.'

As Danny ended the communication with Kinloch, Hoynes rushed from the wheelhouse. 'Right, Hamish. Get back in there and give it all she's got.'

'There's no rush, is there?' replied the bemused first mate.

'Och, the boys are getting right restless below. We'll need to get to oor destination as quickly as we can. Give me a shout when we're close. It can be a tricky wee bay to negotiate.'

Hamish watched Hoynes hurry off, wondering what was in fact the real reason behind the sudden haste. But as his skipper had requested, he grabbed the wheel then throttled the *Girl Maggie* forward. Soon she was making nine knots.

'Is that it?' said Danny, unimpressed by the slight increase in speed.

'Och no, we'll get a knot or two mair once she's got going. Given a fair wind, that is.' Hamish stared out over the calm sea as black smoke belched from the tiny funnel, praying the engine would take the strain.

'I better lash myself to the mast, then.' Danny grinned.

10

A gathering of bemused seals looked on as the *Girl Maggie*, a very small wave at her prow and a very large column of black smoke behind her, slowly turned into the bay. Their heads poked up from the still waters as they looked at each other in silent communion before, as one, disappearing back to the depths. It was clear that these creatures of the sea did not like the look of the fishing boat.

Hoynes, as though by some sixth sense, forced himself through the hatch and made his way to the wheelhouse.

'I'll take over from here, Hamish. We need to get ashore and up to the bothy before sunset. There's nothing worse than a shoal of inebriated fishermen trying to find their wae aboot on land in the dark. A recipe for disaster, and no mistake.'

He took the wheel, pulled back the vessel's modest speed and made a wide sweep across the bay before turning the *Girl Maggie* towards the shore.

'You're no' going to beach her, are you, Sandy?' Hamish looked worried.

'Indeed I am not. But there's a nasty wee set o' rocks at the head o' the bay thonder. Aye, many a mariner has come to grief at this very point. Why dae you think it's called the Smuggler's Hole?'

'I'd no idea that's what it was called.'

'There, you see. The ignorance o' the young. Many a time in decades gone by, fine seamen would put in here when being pursued by the authorities.' Hoynes slowed the vessel to a crawl. 'Just ahead is a convenient sandbank. We'll glide into that, fair brushing it like a feather. Then we need to make our way over the side, and Bob's your uncle.'

Hamish thought for a moment. 'We'll get soaked!'

'You're mother should have called you Thomas. The name would have served you well. Have I ever let you down in matters nautical?'

Hamish bit his lip at this question, recalling several times when the skipper's nautical theories had in fact been somewhat open to question, as the *Girl Maggie*, her engine now disengaged, bumped softly to a stop.

'There, you see. Like powdering a wean's backside.'

'What would you know aboot such things, Sandy?'

'I'm a father of many year's standing. There's nothing Dr Spock can teach me aboot weans, and that's a fact.'

Hamish, clueless, shook his head. He looked over the side into the clear water below.

'You'll be seeing the sandbank now?'

'Aye, but thon water looks cold.'

'You'll have to toughen up, young man. You'll witness these old seadogs fair throwing themselves o'er the side wae gay abandon. The water's no more than a foot deep, and we've all got our seaboots on. Sometimes I wonder if you shouldna be behind a plough rather than a ship's wheel.'

One by one, Hoynes watched his passengers emerge through the hatch, all with less difficulty than himself, he noted with dismay. Yet again, he resolved to have the offending hatch widened at the earliest opportunity. He wasn't remotely concerned that he'd put on a few pounds. Most of the poor souls he visited at Kinloch's cottage hospital were pinched-faced, emaciated souls heading for the unknown waters of oblivion. To Hoynes, an ample girth was a sign of rude health, despite his doctor's advice. What did he know? The man smoked cigarettes by the dozen, and every fool knew that while a pipe was a healthy aid to meditation, cigarettes were lung-choking offences to nature.

Peeny looked over the side. 'Aye, you made a grand job o' that, Sandy. I couldna have done better myself. You just kissed the sandbank like a fair maiden's cheek.'

'If he was going round kissing fair maidens, I'm sure the constabulary would be involved,' said McKirdy, somewhat uncharitably.

'Sheer jealousy,' said Hoynes. 'The time we came here on your old tub we damn near ended up in the trees thonder, such was the rate you ploughed into the bay. It was like watching wee Jackie Stewart take a bend, so it was. My neck was sore for a fortnight.'

As the gloaming began to settle over Absdale Bay, fishermen young and old gathered their possessions – mainly fresh underpants and whisky – and made their way nimbly over the side of the *Girl Maggie*.

Peeny was the first to set foot on the sandbank, having made his way down the narrow rope ladder, kitbag slung over his shoulder. Despite his small stature, as Hoynes had predicted, the water was just below the top of his seaboots. He waded along the sandbank and onto the shingle shore as Hoynes lowered the anchor with a splash.

As, one by one, the seasoned mariners went over the side,

very soon, only Hamish and Hoynes were left aboard.

'Make sure you've switched off that contraption, Hamish. We don't want the damned thing self-combusting in the middle o' the night and leaving us wae only charred timbers instead o' the fine vessel that got us here. I'll get myself onto the sandbank and wait for you.'

Hamish looked on as, not without a little difficulty, Hoynes made his way onto the rope ladder and, red-faced, struggled down onto the sandbank. The first mate made sure that everything was secure and in order aboard, before hauling himself over the side. Though he'd used the rope ladder on many occasions, the passage of seaboots had made the rope slick, and just as he reached the penultimate rung, his foot slipped. Hamish, his kitbag pulling him backwards, fell into the shallow water, right at Hoynes's feet.

The skipper cursed as he brushed the splash of seawater from his beige duffel coat. 'Man, but you're like an elephant on a tightrope, Hamish. All these old boys doon here as lithe as you like, and you taking a dive like an arthritic dolphin. I'm right ashamed, for you've besmirched the good name o' oor vessel.' He waded off along the sandbank in high dudgeon, leaving his first mate, dripping wet, to get back to his feet. The sound of laughter echoed round the small bay as, muttering under his breath, Hamish followed his companions onto the shore.

The little party threaded its way up the beach and into a covering of fir trees. They followed a path which meandered its way up a low rise that became steeper as they progressed. Fortunately, the passage of time and many booted feet had dug little footholds into the bank, so the going wasn't as hard as it might have been. However, bringing up the rear and still shivering following his immersion, Hamish grew increasingly miserable and began to doubt the wisdom of his participation in this trip.

But, as he reached the top of the steep rise, his spirits were lifted by the site of a small wooden construction in a clearing. He turned to look back through the trees and could see the *Girl Maggie* resting safely at anchor below. It was then he realised how well named Smuggler's Hole was. From his position, he could see out into the sound, but any vessel passing by would be unable to see into the sheltering bay. Undoubtably, any craft berthed there was, in effect, invisible. And with the bothy blending in with the trees all around, the place made for the perfect lookout.

The old hut was musty and rustic, but cosy in its own way. Three sets of double bunks adorned by lumpy mattresses and woollen sea blankets were placed along the walls. Three iron camp beds – no doubt liberated at the end of the war – stood against a wall, ready to accommodate surplus guests. At the far corner was a fireplace, already filled with peat, sea coal and logs. Beside it sat two scuttles bearing more fuel and kindling. A few wooden chairs were scattered around.

'Munro's as good as his word, as always,' said Malcolm Connelly. 'Always makes sure we have a fire set for oor arrival and aired blankets.'

'Never misses a year, and him retired from the fishing near as long as you, Andy,' said Hoynes.

'No' quite,' said Andy Duncan. 'But he's always been a fine fellow, and what a man for finding fish! I hear he still goes out from time to time when the fleet at Firdale is struggling for a catch.'

'Somebody better light the damned thing before young

Hamish shivers tae death,' said McKirdy.

Sure enough, in the corner of the room, Hamish's face had taken on a particularly blue hue.

While Danny got busy with the fire, Peeny set a match to the oil lantern that hung in the small-paned window. In minutes the gloomy room was illuminated by jumping flames and the bright flicker of the lantern.

Hamish made for the fire and soon its warmth made him feel more human. Indeed, he felt as though the whole evening was looking up.

Feeling slightly guilty for admonishing his first mate after his fall, Hoynes handed Hamish a tin mug, half-filled with whisky. 'There, get that doon you. I've a spare pair o' dungarees rolled up in my kitbag. They'll no' be neat on you, but they'll do while your own gear dries.'

Hamish smiled. 'Thanks, skipper. Much appreciated. I'm fair looking forward to the night. It'll be time for yarns and a convivial dram or two, I've no doubt.'

Hoynes hesitated. 'Aye, first we've to do that favour. You know, the bales from our friend the farmer.' He winked at Hamish in the firelight.

'You mean, we go back out?'

'Aye, just me and you. Och, it'll take minutes. Once your clothes are dry, we'll be about it.'

'I'll no' manage all those bales myself, Sandy.' Hamish sounded alarmed, recalling his efforts at the farm and back at the *Girl Maggie*.

'You're a right worrier. It's all taken care of, trust me.'

As the fire warmed his backside, a chill ran down Hamish's spine. For when Sandy Hoynes said 'trust me', rarely did it bode well.

11

Collector Alan Marshall looked from the wheelhouse of the cutter *Diane*, as the sun set in cold hues of purple, green and fading gold. Their sail down the Firth of Clyde had been as splendid as it had been speedy. The twin-engine vessel had made short work of the journey from Glasgow on a glorious winter's day, the white-capped hills of Argyll making for a spectacular backdrop.

He cast his binoculars around their new anchorage with an inquisitive, practised eye, aware of the light tread of his second-in-command, John 'Jocky' Cummings behind him. A veteran of this coast, having served for many years in one of the steam puffers that had plied their trade for so long amongst the islands and peninsulas of the West Coast, before opting for a more predictable income, he was a solid, dependable and wise colleague.

'Excuse me, sir, but I'm a wee bit confused,' said Cummings as he stroked his well-trimmed beard.

'Are you, indeed? Why so?' replied Marshall, not taking the binoculars from his eyes.

'Well, it's just that you had me plot the passage to Kinloch. I even informed the harbour master there that we would be seeking a berth on our arrival. But you seem happy to be anchored here in Lochranza, sir.'

Marshall let the binoculars hang by the leather strap round his neck. He took a deep breath of sea air as he regarded the castle on the point of the small jutting headland within the bay. 'I've always liked it here on Arran. Scotland in miniature, they say, and an honest, hard-working populace into the bargain.'

'You'll be meaning unlike the parcel o' rogues in Kinloch?'

'Aye, something like that, Jocky. But isn't it grand to be back at sea? I spend far too much time these days stuck at my desk. It's not a healthy life.'

'But a productive one, sir. If we weren't here to keep tabs on some of the freebooters that sail these waters, the Revenue would suffer the consequences, and no mistake.'

'You've answered your own question.'

'How so, sir?'

'Well, I told you about the tip-off we had first thing this morning. Having you book us a berth at Kinloch was no more than a *ruse de guerre*.'

Getting his superior's intention without necessarily picking up on the French, Cummings nodded sagely. 'I see, sir. You're quite right, of course. You can't trust a body down in Kinloch not to broadcast the slightest detail of anything going on.'

'Including the harbour master.'

'Most definitely. I remember I fell into the hold when we were hauling coal onto the quay at Bowmore on Islay – I was eighteen. Broke my wrist, so I did, though the doctor there did a passable job at setting it.' Cummings flexed his left wrist to prove the statement. 'That was late afternoon on a Tuesday. We sailed for Kinloch first thing the next morning. Man, every bugger and his friend knew what had happened to me – the circumstances, treatment and even the name of the doctor who attended me – by the time we tied up at the pier.'

'I don't doubt it. I worked there for two years. It only took them a matter of days to find out where I was from, what church I attended and my wife's maiden name. I'm quite sure they knew more than me about her antecedence, and that's a fact.'

'If ever there was a place where a local newspaper was surplus to requirements, it's Kinloch, and no mistake. I still can't work out how they do it.'

'Ah, but such free-flowing knowledge can work both ways, Jocky. It's easy to throw a spanner in the works of a good tale.' Marshall reached for his pipe. 'Our quarry will have heard of our imminent arrival at Kinloch. Had they not heard this, the grubby transaction I reckon is about to take place would have been risked in daylight. But now, knowing we're abroad, our perpetrators will no doubt seek the cover of darkness.'

'True, sir, very true.'

'But as we know, nothing can be done in the dark without recourse to lights of some kind. During the day, we could sit off the peninsula and easily miss wrongdoers. But a clandestine light is easily spotted at night, wouldn't you say?'

'Oh, I agree wholeheartedly, sir.'

'So, that's what we're going to do. We'll stay here until dark then make way into the sound. With the radar at our disposal, we'll be fine to leave off our own lights. A few good men with binoculars is all that's required. We'll have a great vantage point to see almost from Firdale to the head of the loch. At the first sign of any unusual, suspicious light, we'll make for its source at full speed.'

'Very cunning, sir, if I may say so.'

'You have to be cunning to catch whisky smugglers, Jocky. And from what I hear, this won't be an insignificant haul.

Plus, we'll bring a man to justice who has been a thorn in our side for many years.'

Cummings mulled over this for a moment as the light leached from the sky over the line of houses, the hotel and shops of Lochranza. 'Would you mind if I ventured a guess at the name of your quarry, sir?'

Marshall turned to his number two with a curious expression. 'Be my guest. I'll be interested to hear if you get it right. In fact, a dram for you on me when we bring the bugger to book.'

'It'll be Sandy Hoynes, I'm thinking.'

'Ha!' Marshall clapped Cummings on the shoulder. 'That's a large whisky I owe you, Jocky!'

'He's a slippery one, sir. I've known him since I was no more than a lad. I think his record is as clean as the driven snow.'

'By tomorrow it'll be well tainted, Jocky. You have my word.'

12

A sickle moon shone brightly before a carpet of stars, the sweep of the Milky Way silhouetting the bothy amongst the fir trees, as the world turned. Only the pale flicker of the oil lamp in the window spilled yellow light onto the path as the revellers, set to bring in the Auld New Year, warmed themselves up with stories and the tinny sound of fiddle music from an old wireless. The bothy was warm now, notes of burning peat adding to the heady tang of the whisky with which each man nurtured his soul.

Hoynes, quieter than was his habit, reached for his pocket watch. With the hour nearing seven, he calculated what was to be done. He reckoned that if he and Hamish went about their business in half an hour or so, they should be able to return to the festivities well before ten of the clock.

Peeny was busy with a shaggy dog's tale of a man from Tarbert who'd eaten a whole bicycle for a bet. Hoynes had heard the story before, but its delivery was nonetheless entertaining.

'The last bit he'd to swallow was the bell,' said Peeny, as the company looked on, enthralled.

'A hellish mouthful,' opined Connelly.

'He'd just eaten the frame, wheels and the handlebar,' replied the storyteller indignantly. 'The bell presented no obstacle. But there was a catch, mind you.'

'Isn't there always? I've never known anyone in Tarbert go about anything in a straightforward manner.' There was a mumble of agreement from the gathered Kinloch fishermen, who, to a man, regarded the fishing port at the northernmost end of the Kintyre peninsula with the utmost suspicion.

'Aye, every time he moved, from that day on, you can hear the bell ring as though it was still attached to the bike. Ding-ding, all day every day. Can you imagine?'

'Ach, wheesht, man. I've never heard the like,' said Andy Duncan.

'I tell you, it's true!' Peeny thumped the bowl of his briar pipe on the arm of his chair by way of affirmation. 'The whole escapade cost him dear, for though he won the bet, he suffered terribly. For a start, his wife couldna bear all that ringing when they were going about their conjugal procedures. It fair put her off the notion, right enough. She ended up running off wae a man travelling in fancy goods fae Paisley. Aye, and that wasn't the worst o' it.'

'You don't say,' said McKirdy.

'No, not by a long chalk. He lost his berth at the fishing – understandably, you'll agree. Who'd want a man aboard that rings wae every step? Even if you could thole it, the fish would take fair exception to the racket.' He paused for effect as everyone considered this. 'In any event, he took to a life o' crime in order to keep body and soul together. Och, it was petty stuff at first, a bit o' shoplifting and the likes. He was helped by the fact that every time he dinged, the shopkeeper looked to the door, and oor man was free to fill his pockets. But it soon got worse. His career as a criminal ended up at a bank somewhere in Glasgow. Armed robbery, no less.'

'For any's sake,' said Danny, his mouth agape.

'Aye, he and this other bloke were caught in the act. The Tarbert fella made a bolt for it up a close. But you know fine how sharp the polis in Glasgow are. They'd clocked the ringing. So, two stout bobbies just hung aboot in the shadows until oor man decided the coast was clear. He was no sooner oot into the street before half the polis in the city descended on him. The poor bugger got eight years for his troubles.'

Those taken with the story shook their heads at the plight of their fellow fisherman, while the more sceptical – including Hoynes – merely raised their eyes to the ceiling and took another sip of whisky.

'He was back oot in five for good behaviour,' said Peeny. 'Man, I was up in Tarbert when I saw him last. The poor soul had aged twenty years.'

'How did you recognise him?' enquired young Danny.

'His face was wrinkled and drawn, hair sparse and grey. But the fact he was ringing all the way down the street fair gave him away.' Peeny winked at the older and wiser members of the company, as the more gullible wondered at this sorry tale. 'They tell me he passed away not long ago. No doubt the result o' all that time spent in the jail, no' to mention the unhealthy aftermath o' eating a whole bicycle.'

'Poor bugger,' said Danny with a shake of the head.

'Mind you, they say his son's a dead ringer for him.' Peeny managed to keep his face straight as he finished his tale.

The laughter that filled the bothy was halted by a sharp knock at the door.

Hoynes was first to his feet. 'That sounds right official, does it no'?'

'Like the polis,' whispered McMichael.

'Or worse still, the fishery officer,' croaked Andy Duncan.

Hoynes straightened up and headed for the door, his heart thudding in his chest at the thought of the cargo in the hold of the *Girl Maggie*.

'Who's there abroad at this time o' night?' he called.

'It's me,' came a muffled voice from behind the door.

'That's all very well, but I'm no' right sure who "me" is,' replied Hoynes.

'Munro!'

The sing-song Highland voice of the Firdale fisherman put Hoynes at his ease. Recovering from his palpitations, he opened the door wide for the man who'd left them peat, coal, logs and fresh bedding. 'Come in, come in,' said Hoynes. 'We owe you a few bumpers and a bite to eat at the very least for your kindness.'

Munro appeared from the shadows of night into the flickering warmth of the bothy.

'You're as pale as a ghost,' said Connelly, staring at their guest, a small, spare man with unruly grey hair sticking up from his round head.

'I'm sorry to be a nuisance, lads. I know this is a Kinloch thing, but I've just had a bad experience.'

Hamish, still clad in Hoynes's more than ample dungarees, ushered Munro into the chair he'd been occupying.

The Firdale man smelled strongly of the cold outdoors from which he'd just emerged. 'Thank you, son, much appreciated.'

'Here,' said Hoynes, pushing a large glass of whisky into their unexpected visitor's trembling hand. 'That should warm the cockles nicely.'

'Kind of you, Sandy, most kind, indeed. Man, what a fright I've had. I'll no' forget this night in a hurry.'

'Don't leave us wondering, Mr Munro,' said Hamish.

'Well, this morning I had a visit from MacIntosh, the gamekeeper. Yous will likely know who I mean?' Munro looked around to nods of recognition. 'He's babysitting they hens for the Absdale Estate.'

'A finer egg canna be consumed,' said Hoynes. 'The creamiest yolk you'll ever sample – even if they do have a tint o' green aboot them, which is unfortunate.'

'You're right, Sandy. But that's no' the gist o' the story.' He took a gulp of whisky. 'MacIntosh telt me aboot an experience he had last night. There's been poachers aboot, you see. He had his eyes and ears fair peeled in case they tried to make away wae the hens, for there's folk far and wide would like to set hands on them.'

'I'm no' so sure you can peel your ain ears, Munro,' said Hoynes thoughtfully. 'But carry on while I ponder on the matter.'

'You'll no' be worried aboot what can or can't be done wae ears when you hear this, Sandy. Anyhow, MacIntosh thought he heard the drip o' oars. As yous will know, these poachers are fly buggers and they make sure their rowlocks are muffled when they're about their business.'

'You canna trust a man wae muffled rowlocks, and no error,' said McKirdy, caught up with the serious nature of this news.

'MacIntosh cracks together his gun, ready for action, and he hides in the bushes beyond the beach. He's a fearless man, and I'm sure he'd no' hesitate to shoot anyone aboot to interfere with his birds.'

'Aye, and quite right,' observed Andy Duncan.

Munro took another draw at his whisky. His face, flushed by the heat in the room and the spirit, became suddenly pale.

'Well, as it turns out, he was right aboot the oars. But these were no poachers.'

'It surely wasn't the Kilmartin rowing club at that time o' night?' said Hoynes.

'Was it the fishery officer?' said McKirdy, the remark predicated upon the notion that the appearance of said official could be the only reason behind the fearful look on the Firdale fisherman's face.

'No fishery officer nor rowing club. It was a Viking longship – men at the oars, fire burning fore and aft from braziers, and a menacing figure at the prow. Like a nightmare.' Munro stared into the fire. 'Damn me, but did this bugger no' call oot to MacIntosh, and him concealed behind a bush.'

'What kind o' bush?' asked Peeny.

'Och, that's irrelevant, man' said Munro. 'Let me get on wae the tale, will you?'

Hoynes drained his glass and all but fell into a chair. Hamish noticed this with puzzlement, that and his skipper's unusual reticence on the subject. For, as the first mate had experienced, Sandy Hoynes was not a man who kept his opinions to himself – under normal circumstances, at least.

'This MacIntosh must tell a fine tale, eh? The colour of you sitting there, a body would swear you'd seen this ghostly vessel yourself,' said Peeny.

The older man looked blankly into his face and raised a bony finger. 'That's the thing. I've just witnessed the very same apparition. I was heading here to make sure all was well, rounded the point on the path and was making my way up the wee hill . . .' His eyes widened. 'I don't know what it was that made me turn – perhaps the hairs on the back o' my neck, perhaps another sense o' which I'm no' aware – I canna be sure. But turn I did. Down in the bay, just yards away from Sandy's boat, there it was. Long, sleek, the figure of a snake picked out by firelight at the prow.'

A disconcerted mumble passed its way amongst the Kinloch company. For, to a man, they were creatures of the sea. And every one of them knew that the laws of nature enjoyed by the land-bound didn't apply to those who took to the ocean for a living. In a storm, in dead calm or a sea mist, they had all experienced things that rarely formed part of the yarns for which fishermen are rightly famous. Things so troubling they were beyond frivolity. Each of them had felt a chill hand on the heart, but more often than not, such events were more a sensation, a feeling, rather than the full-blown experience that Munro had just described. All the same, these occurrences were best not discussed, fishing being a dangerous enough occupation without the addition of the supernatural.

Peeny pursed his lips. In Kinloch, such a story would be banished to whispers and nights when whisky flowed all too freely. Kinloch fishermen, regardless of the contents of their hearts, were practical men, not given to fancy – not in public, at any rate. 'You boys fae Firdale are always prone to the wind-up. Many a tall tale I've heard at the hotel in the village. If you've come to spook us, you'll find a poor audience.' He laughed, but there was something hollow in the sound that made it somehow disingenuous.

'Aye, come on, Munro. We're no' a parcel o' daft wee boys – well, apart fae Hamish and young Danny o'er there,' said McKirdy.

'I'm near thirty!' Hamish protested.

'But that mother of yours would still have you in short trousers if they made them in a suitable size,' said Peeny.

He'd hoped to engender some humour back into the proceedings, but with Munro looking pale and greatly unsettled, the response was a thin snigger rather than the belly laugh for which he'd hoped.

It took Hoynes to break the spell. 'Right, Vikings or no', me and Hamish have a wee errand to be getting on with. It shouldna take us more than an hour or so. I'll leave you to tales o' the Norsemen.' He nodded to his first mate. 'Your gear will be dry by now. You better get oot o' they dungarees o' mine and get yoursel' shipshape.' Hoynes lit his pipe as Hamish sloped off into the shadows to change his clothes.

'And what are you at, eh?' said Andy Duncan, his weatherbeaten face sombre after the tale they'd just been told.

'Nothing at all. A wee favour for a friend o' mine just up the coast a bit. His auld auntie died a month back. She left him a fine piece of furniture. I think they call them Welsh dressers – a grand thing it is, at any rate. I said I'd drop it off earlier, but damn me, did it no' just slip my mind, what wae all the excitement at being abroad wae all you fine fellows.'

Peeny stroked his stubbly chin. 'I had a notion the *Girl Maggie* was sitting low in the water. Had I not known better I'd have thought that you'd a fair catch aboard.'

Hoynes brushed this aside with a wave of his pipe. 'You're forgetting I'd passengers. And some o' you aren't at your fighting weight, I think it's fair to say.'

As Peeny raised his brow, Munro looked up from the flames of the fire, his expression still haunted. 'You're no' taking to the water after what I've just told you, surely, Sandy?'

'I'm a man o' little fear, as you all know fine. And, to be fair, I'd rather meet up wae a Viking than the fishery officer any day of the week.' Hoynes laughed heartily at his own observation. But when he turned away from the little huddle of fishermen, his face, shadowed in the dancing flames of the fire, took on a deadly serious expression.

13

Now out in the sound, Marshall, Cummings and the three crewmembers of the Revenue cutter had their eyes focused on the length of the east Kintyre coast. Each man was searching for the tiniest glimmer of light from the many bays and inlets that dotted the peninsula. Though Marshall's memory of the area had diminished with the years, he knew Cummings had every part of the place off by heart. In short, with a powerful engine and the inside knowledge that had sparked the mission from the outset, they were well placed to bring wrongdoers to justice.

The night, though, was still. The stars arched over the sound in a magnificent display, but the only other lights to be seen were those of the lighthouses on the Cock of Arran and the distant Ayrshire coast.

'Nothing yet, sir,' said Cummings, his duffel coat buttoned up tight at his throat and a stout scarf wound about his neck.

'There's time aplenty,' replied Marshall. 'Hoynes will appear when we least expect it, you'll see. From what I remember, and the reports I've been reading today, the man has a talent for surprise.'

'There can be little doubt about that, sir. A wilier mariner there has never been – with the exception of that Raleigh fella, pirates and the like. And they've no' set sail for a goodly number of years.'

'I can just see Hoynes at the helm of a privateer. He has the looks for it.'

'He was more akin to Father Christmas the last time I saw him, right enough. He's carrying a fair cargo o' timber round the belly these days. Aye, and his beard's as white as his hair.'

Marshall took his eyes from his binoculars, surprised by this information. It was strange how people changed. When one saw an individual on a regular basis physical change was so gradual it barely registered. But encountering someone for the first time in years was bound to be a surprise. Reflecting on his own appearance, he realised that the flecks of grey at his temples and the wrinkles around his eyes hadn't been there when he worked in Kinloch so long ago. In fact, he'd considered himself rather suave and sophisticated in his trench coat and trilby hat back then. But fashions had changed, and in common with most other middle-aged men, Marshall thought less of his appearance and more of comfort, as the wearing of the warm Toorie that was pulled low down over his forehead proved.

He was still ruminating on the subject of age and the changes it engendered when there was a call from one of the crew.

'Sir, look to port – I'm sure I can see lights.'

Both Marshall and Cummings swivelled their binoculars in the appropriate direction.

'Well done, Frazer. I see them,' said Marshall.

'Confirmed,' agreed Cummings.

'Right, the chase is on. Engage the engines and steer for those lights at full speed, Mr Cummings!'

The deep growl of the powerful engines banished the silence of the cold night. In a few minutes, the cutter was making her way to port, a foaming wave at her bow translucent in the darkness.

Hamish followed his skipper down the narrow path towards the *Girl Maggie*, the roll neck of his thick sea jumper pulled over his chin. The air was frosty, the smell of the fire burning in the bothy overlaying the tang of the sea and the earthy notes of the land.

The younger man cast his eye first to the bay, then out into the sound. But there was no sign of a Viking longship, just the stout figure of their broad-beamed vessel nestling under the lee of the sandbank. The tide had receded now, and the sand next to which the fishing boat wallowed shone silver in the starlight, like a celestial path.

'At least you'll manage to stay dry this time,' said Hoynes, the pale smoke of his pipe billowing into the air.

'You're right sore on me, Sandy. That ladder was slick – any man could have come a cropper.'

'If you say so. But, mind, men more than twice your age navigated it with ease, Hamish.'

The first mate mumbled something under his breath then decided to change the subject. In truth, though he knew of the hay bales and the lemonade bottles filled with whisky, he'd supposed that they'd have been taken to their destination the following day. He hadn't reckoned on the convivial atmosphere of the bothy being interrupted by this covert jaunt. And though he'd always suspected that there was something 'below decks' about the whole enterprise, he was now sure that the *Girl Maggie*'s cargo was less than lawful. 'What will I be getting for my trouble this night, skipper?'

Hoynes stopped his progress down the bank and turned to face his first mate. 'What on earth do you mean?'

'I reckon you'll be getting a good wee cut of whatever it is we're to be up to. I should surely get my share.'

'You'll remember that you have a half share o' the working finances o' this vessel. We're merely doing a favour for the much put-upon folk o' Firdale. Every man deserves a recreational dram at a reasonable price. I thought you would realise that.'

'Even if it comes in lemonade bottles?'

'Now, I explained that to you. Not that I needed to, mind. Remember. *If I can help my fellow man along the way then my life was not in vain.* That's from the Scriptures, though just what book and verse escapes me at the moment.'

They made their way onto the sandbank. It took Hoynes a couple of goes to lift himself onto the rope ladder, but with remarkable speed he was soon over the side and back aboard the *Girl Maggie*, Hamish in his wake.

'Do you reckon she'll come off all right, Sandy?'

'Och, I daresay a day sailor would have his work cut out. But I could get us back out into the sound wae my eyes closed. You get down and fire up the engine, Hamish. The sooner we get about this mission o' mercy, the quicker we'll be back amidst the warmth and celebrations.'

'There wasna much in the way o' celebrations going on, as far as I could see. Just a parcel o' auld sea dogs blethering – aye, and Peeny's tall tales. Would we no' just as well be at the County?'

'Man, you've let the free love turn your mind, Hamish. There's mair to life than propping up the bar at the County, as you'll find out as you get older, I hope. I'd hate to picture you as one o' the old soaks that bide in there, fair shaking their empty glasses in the hope someone will be good enough to stand them a replenishment. No life at all.'

'Don't be daft. When I'm that age, I'll likely be dandling some grandweans on my knee.'

'In that case, you'd better get a shift on. You don't go straight to the grandweans – the weans come first. And if you don't mind me saying, you're no' making much progress on that front.'

Hamish looked suitably aggrieved by this comment, choosing only to grunt in response.

'Maybe the Auld Stones will put lead in your pencil. They can work all manner o' miracles.'

'The Auld Stones?'

Hoynes hurried to the wheelhouse. 'Och, I've no' the time to enlighten you at the moment. We have an errand o' mercy to be at. You'll find oot soon enough.'

'And what aboot these Vikings, Sandy?' Hamish laughed.

Hoynes spun on the heel of his seaboot. 'You'd do well not tae mock, Hamish. Aye, none o' us know what we think we know, and that's a fact.' He opened the door of the wheelhouse, and soon the lantern hanging in that small space flickered into life.

14

As anyone with the slightest knowledge of Scotland's West Coast will acknowledge, the weather can change in an instant. And this night was no different. No sooner had Marshall set off in search of his prey, than a mist began to envelop the vessel. The nearer to the coast of Kintyre they sailed, the thicker it became.

'Damn!' exclaimed Marshall. 'Where has this come from?'

'Not unheard o' in cold weather like this, sir. Och, it's likely a freezing fog. They can be damnable tricky, right enough.'

'Just as well we've the radar to rely on.' Marshall played with a toggle on his duffel coat, deep in thought. 'In fact, it may be a blessing in disguise. They'll never know where we are now, and we'll see any vessel that moves. There won't be many honest folk abroad on a night like this, eh?'

'I'd reckon not, sir. And it's the old New Year. That still holds in these parts, in certain communities, at least.'

'Good grief. The Dark Ages, to be sure.' Marshall checked the radar. By his reckoning, they were less than a mile from where the lights had been spotted, but the green sweep of the screen showed no sign of any vessel. 'Right, let's linger here a while. Cut the engine. We'll keep our eye on this.'

'It's not as though we can see much else, that's for sure.'

'You have the right of it there, Jocky. Who'd have thought this would come down so quickly?'

Hoynes eyed the sudden fog with disdain. 'Would you credit it, Hamish? The night was as clear as a bell – man, you could see Venus. Now I canna see the prow.'

'It's bad luck, right enough, Sandy. Should we leave the bay?'

'Some things have to be done, and this task won't wait.'

'Can we no' jeest drop off the cargo tomorrow? It's no' as though we'd be going far out of our way.'

'Och no, that wouldn't be a good idea at all. For a start, the fishery officer could get wind o' the whole thing and take umbrage.'

'Surely he's no' interested in hay bales.' Hamish looked for Hoynes's reaction from the corner of his eye.

'These buggers are into everything – don't ever doubt it. You could be dropping off the Queen by special appointment and the fishery officer would want her weighed, verified and accounted for, and that's a fact.'

'Anyway, we should be mair worried aboot the Ministry of Agriculture, the amount o' hay we're carrying.'

'Just you wheesht. I've tae navigate oot o' here in a pea-souper. Take note and watch an expert at his trade. It's the only way to learn.' Hoynes tugged at the wheel as the tone of the old diesel engine rose. 'You see, it's all up here.' He tapped his temple. 'When nature deprives you o' your senses, you've only your heid to do the seeing. Now, if I was just any sailor, we'd likely be—' Hoynes didn't get to finish his sentence. The *Girl Maggie* came to a sudden and unceremonious stop, throwing both of them forward in the wheelhouse. Hoynes's pipe, clenched between his teeth, was sent flying, its owner cursing.

'What happened?' said Hamish.

'You go and take a gander over the side while I find my pipe.'

Hamish did as he was told. Picking up a torch from the wheelhouse, he ventured into the mist. It was so thick that he had to shine its faded beam down at his feet, just in case he fell over a net. As he directed it over the side, he frowned at the sight. Carefully, he made his way back to Hoynes.

'Is it a stray log or the like, Hamish?'

'Man, it would have to be a fair-sized log to bring us to such a standstill, Sandy. No, it was the sandbank. You must have turned the wheel the wrong way – fair disoriented by the fog, and all.'

Hoynes thought for a moment. He smiled broadly at Hamish. 'Now, let that be a lesson to you. I was waiting for you to correct me, but you were as mute as a wooden horse. You'll need to pay more attention if you're to skipper a fine vessel like this.'

'So, the fact we went the wrong way was my fault?'

'Merely testing your faculties, Hamish. They're clearly no' up to much. Now, lesson over, I'll get us out into the sound. You could help by giving that sandbank a prod wae the boathook. Aye, this'll be a night you won't forget in a hurry.'

Hamish left the wheelhouse and raised his eyes to the heavens. He always marvelled at the elaborate excuses Hoynes could concoct to cover his deficiencies. He'd heard politicians on the wireless desperately trying to cover their tracks following some blunder or other. They should seek out my skipper for advice, he always thought.

Just as Hamish reached for the boathook, something caught his eye. For a moment, he was sure that an orange flash crossed his line of sight. He peered into the fog, but there was nothing to be seen.

Marshall stared into the radar screen. He was beginning to doubt his own reasoning now. Perhaps their quarry had given them the slip? The lights they'd seen could quite easily have been a decoy. But, he reasoned, nobody knew where they were, so why employ such tactics? Being a man confident in his own ability, he quickly dismissed the notion and squinted harder at the screen.

He was about to hand the duty over to Cummings when, sure enough, as if from nowhere, the ping of what could only be a vessel appeared, emerging from the coastline like a miracle. 'Cummings, we have them!' Marshall made a rough calculation in his head. 'Steer sixteen degrees to port!'

15

Back at the bothy, the Kinloch contingent were busy trying to console Munro, who was still spooked following his run-in with the spectral longship. Catching McKirdy's attention, Peeny gestured to the door with his pipe.

'I fancy a wee breath o' the night air,' he said. 'Though I love my baccy dearly, wae all of us smoking in such a confined space, I'm no' sure I'm smoking my pipe or McKirdy's.'

'I'll come and, eh, keep you company,' replied McKirdy awkwardly, as though he'd taken time to learn the lines.

They stepped out into the cold night and were immediately taken by the fog that had appeared so unexpectedly.

'Man, this won't help us trek up to the stones,' said Peeny.

'We've time yet. And, mind, we're waiting for Hoynes to come back after delivering his furniture.' McKirdy looked sceptical.

'Furniture! I had young Danny take a look intae the hold when Sandy was busy at one of his yarns. He telt me the boat is fair stowed to the gunnels wae hay bales. That's why she was so low in the water.'

'Hay bales? What on earth for?'

'Your guess is as good as mine. But you can be damned sure the bugger's up to something – and I'll wager it's not farming-related.'

'Och, it's none o' our business, Peeny. As long as he's back in good time for midnight, we canna make comment.'

'It would be oor business if the authorities had happened upon us on the way here, and him wae goodness knows what contraband aboard. Guilty by association, that's what the cry would have been.'

'You surely don't think he's at the smuggling?'

'You hear aboot it all the time these days. The young folk are falling o'er themselves to get a hold o' the drugs, and no mistake. It seems a good dram is of no consequence to the younger generation.'

'Heavens! I've known Sandy pull a few stunts in my time, but this isna a buckshee octopus, or a few extra pounds o' mackerel. They say his daughter is winching the police sergeant. He'll likely have one eye on the wedding. Every ha'penny is a prisoner in that hoose. The poor lassie will likely walk doon the aisle in widow's weeds.'

'Drugs is a serious matter. I've been thinking Hamish has been sampling them for a while. Look at that carry-on at New Year. Aye, and Sandy himself. I'm still no' quite sure what happened in that blizzard before Christmas. But I'd no' be surprised if he was on a trip.'

'Where tae, Peeny?'

'That's what they call it when you're away wae the fairies on the drugs. I didna mean he'd taken the weekend in Edinburgh.'

McKirdy took this in with a grave look. He pictured Sandy Hoynes partaking in the opium he'd read about in novels. But somehow, he couldn't reconcile the mental image. 'Where would he get the time? He's either out at sea at the fishing or he's in the County Hotel wae the rest o' us.'

'The man's likely up half the night abusing himself. It's Marjorie I feel sorry for.'

Again, a mental image formed in McKirdy's mind's eye. But it was so alarming he felt a change of conversation was warranted. 'What are your thoughts on Munro's ramblings? You don't reckon he's taken to the drugs and all, do you?'

'He's fae Firdale. They'll have all manner o' hallucinations in that place. Quite common, I should say. They reckon that half o' the village are by-blows o' the sailors fae the Spanish Armada. That's a trauma that would go down the centuries. It's a wonder it wisna auld King Henry he was seeing.'

'He beheaded all o' his wives.'

'Munro? The bad bugger.'

'No, auld King Henry. I'm sure you don't get off wae beheading these days – even in Firdale. But, thinking on it, I reckon that Elizabeth was on the throne at the time o' the Armada.'

Peeny looked unconvinced as he stared around in the dense mist. 'I wonder how many souls spent their days in this place, eh?'

'The village?'

'Aye. They say the last body that lived here went mad wae isolation. That was well o'er a hundred years ago. Their rough auld cottages are nothing more than a heap o' ruins now. It makes you wonder.'

'Wonder what?'

'Who'll remember us when we're gone?'

McKirdy pondered upon this as he puffed on his pipe. 'They might no' remember us, but I'm willing tae bet they remember Sandy Hoynes.'

16

Marshall could almost smell the success. The more he thought about it, the more he could remember his time in Kinloch. The image and reputation of Sandy Hoynes became clearer, the closer they came to the vessel, which was now picked out brightly on the radar screen.

'We should be in hailing distance of them within five minutes, sir,' said Cummings.

'We'll use the Tannoy. It normally scares the life out of these miscreants. That's the one good thing about this mist. They won't see us coming. I don't believe Hoynes will be equipped with radar.'

'I hear he only purchased a radio a wee while ago. The authorities forced it on him after that caper before Christmas in the blizzards. You'll remember it was in all the papers, sir.'

'That was Hoynes? My goodness, I hadn't realised.'

'Aye, he's quite the celebrity, these days – in Kinloch, at any rate.'

'We'll soon put a stop to that. Let people see the real man behind the myth, eh? Slow the engine, Cummings. We want this to be as big a surprise as possible.'

✧

Meanwhile, all was not well aboard the *Girl Maggie*. Sandy Hoynes still couldn't find his pipe, and Hamish had taken a tumble amidships and was now sporting a bruise visibly burgeoning from his forehead.

'Don't take a smoke, Hamish. It's the very worst thing you can do wae an injury such as the one you've just sustained.'

'Why so, Sandy?'

'Ach, the baccy fair aggravates the trauma. Hand me your pipe and keep a weather eye on the coast. You should see a swaying light on the shore. That's the signal.'

'Signal for what?'

'Signal for us to heave-to and get rid o' all this hay.'

'I'll be hard-pressed to see anything through this mist, Sandy. And for discussion's sake, the word "signal" has worrisome connotations.'

'It's a word – what are you worried aboot?'

'I read a fair pile o' books when I was a lad. Thon smuggler Red MacEachran was forever looking out for signals.'

'Man, you're heid is fair planted in the clouds, and no error. What do you expect them to do, wave a wee flag? You'll no' see that in the mist, that's for certain. Lights, you can see in the dark; flags are fine in the daylight, but hellish useless at night – especially in a mist. Now, get your glimmers on that shore or you'll have another bruise to match the one you've already got.'

It was at this moment that a number of things appeared to happen simultaneously. No sooner had Hamish turned his attention to the shore than he spotted a light, swaying in the mist, just as Hoynes had described. The first mate turned to his skipper, about to speak, when the silence of the night was shattered by the sudden roar of an amplified voice.

'Stop engines and drop anchor! This is her Majesty's Revenue cutter *Diane*. We intend to board. I repeat: we intend to board.'

Hoynes expressed his feelings with the use of a loud oath, as, for the second time that night, a pipe dropped from his mouth and landed on an undisclosed part of the wheelhouse floor.

'Damn me, Sandy, but we're done for!' wailed Hamish.

For Hoynes, the few split seconds that elapsed seemed like hours, as he desperately sought to find a believable response to the question of why there were a large number of hay bales cosseting lemonade bottles filled with illicit whisky in his hold. But before he could come up with anything suitable, a blazing flash of fire passed before his line of sight.

The sudden rush of flames made Marshall take a step back. 'What on earth? The bloody man has set his vessel on fire!'

Cummings rushed to his side. 'Sir, he's making a run for it. We should pursue. He'll never outrun us in that tub.'

'Yes, get after him! I'm damned if that rascal is going to outsmart us.'

The great engine of the cutter roared once more as Cummings steered towards the flickering flames, now disappearing into the mist. 'I don't know what he's at, sir. If his vessel is on fire, eventually they'll need to abandon ship. What chance will men have in the water in these conditions? They'll freeze to death before we can locate them.'

'Hoynes clearly has no regard for his own safety or that of his crew. The man's more ruthless than we imagined. Make haste, Mr Cummings. There could be lives at stake!'

✧

Hamish looked open-mouthed at Hoynes, as the cutter disappeared back into the mist. 'What on earth happened, Sandy? How did you make that fire appear oot o' nowhere?'

'Och, think nothing of it,' muttered Hoynes. 'You've got to be on your toes for any eventuality, right enough.' Had he been in possession of a pipe on which to draw, he would surely have done so. Instead, he bit his lip as he stared back out to sea. 'We need to get into the shore as quickly as we can, Hamish. You steer to my signal. I'll make my way out on deck and guide you. But mind and keep your lugs open. One mistake and we're beached.'

As Hoynes stumbled out of the wheelhouse, his mind was a tumble of thoughts. When he'd heard the Tannoy from the cutter his blood had run cold. Though he wasn't responsible for the appropriation of the whisky he carried aboard, he'd have faced questions he'd have been unable and unwilling to answer, had the Revenue vessel not taken off after the flames. That thought took him back to only a few short weeks ago. Though his memory was still hazy, muddled by an accidental ingestion of narcotics, he could still picture the handsome longship, braziers burning bright with flame, fore and aft. But it couldn't be; that experience had been chemically induced. The whole escapade had haunted him ever since.

Then there was Munro's tale to take into account. His description of what he'd seen earlier that evening had chimed almost exactly with Hoynes's vision while under the influence.

Now, more than ever, Hoynes was convinced that what he'd seen in the heavy snow was not a drug-fuelled fever dream. But he had more pressing matters to think about now.

Troubled, yet relieved, he looked over the side of the *Girl Maggie* at the lantern swaying on the shore. 'Ahoy!' he shouted. 'Guide me in, and we'll have to get moving!'

Hoynes called to Hamish to steer slowly towards the light. As they neared the shore, the shadows of men, seemingly cut in two, with only their heads and torsos to be seen, emerged like some ghastly vision through the mist.

'What are you taking us into, Sandy?' Hamish's trembling voice issued from the wheelhouse.

'Wheesht, man, and concentrate on what you're doing. When I raise my hand, stop the engine and we'll drift into place.'

The closer the *Girl Maggie* came to the shore, the more obvious it was that the shadows of men weren't the gruesome visions that Hamish had conjured up. Indeed, not far off the beach, as the mist cleared, he could see around twenty figures wading through the waist-height water, each man wearing fishermen's waders. They were dragging something behind them through the waves – a large raft, Hamish quickly realised.

'Stop!' shouted Hoynes, waving one arm in the air to reinforce the point.

Soon, and with admirable speed, men were pouring over the side of the *Girl Maggie* and up the rope ladder like a pirate boarding party. One man whispered to Hoynes, and soon they'd formed three human chains. Men passed hay bales out of the hold and up into the arms of their companions, who then handed them over the side to men on the raft. Hamish was mesmerised by their speed and skill, remembering how long it had taken to load the vessel in the first place.

In minutes, the hay and the whisky were aboard the raft and it was slowly pushed toward the shore. Almost as quickly as they had appeared, one by one, those aboard the fishing boat had disappeared over the side and slipped into the darkness.

'Right, Hamish! Let's get back to Smuggler's Hole. There are celebrations to be had!'

Hamish stepped back to let Hoynes take over the wheel of the *Girl Maggie*. 'I don't know how you did that, Sandy. Man, it was like a military operation.'

'Thirsty men are easy to motivate, Hamish. Those poor buggers in Firdale have throats like camels' feet. Anything can be achieved if the spirit is willing – never forget that.'

'Aye, "spirit" being the operative word.' Hamish thought for a moment. 'It would be you who conjured up the fire to distract the Revenue? How did you manage it?'

Hoynes remained silent for a moment. When he did speak, his voice was almost a whisper. 'Hamish, I'm going to tell you something, but there's two things you must promise me before I do.'

'Aye, I promise.'

'For a start, you must never repeat this to a soul – not even your ain mother.'

'You have my word.'

'But before that, a more pressing task.'

'Aye – just tell me.' Hamish was anxious to hear more as he looked wide-eyed at Hoynes.

'Get yourself down on the floor and find they pipes. I'm fair gasping for a smoke.'

17

It was just after ten, and all talk in the bothy was centred around Sandy Hoynes and his whereabouts. Munro was shaking his head, prophecies of doom on his lips. Meanwhile Connelly, McMichael, McKirdy and Peeny were merely irritated by his absence.

'It's always the same,' said Peeny. 'If there's disturbance to be had, Hoynes is at the heart o' it. He was the same as a boy when he left the school for his father's boat. I'm a couple o' years older, but I remember him fine wae his blond hair and his schemes. Drove his auld fella daft, and that's the truth. Trouble has always followed Sandy like an auld dog.'

Andy Duncan was sitting by the fire, quietly contemplating the flames as they sparked and danced before his old, wrinkled face. At his great age, he had found peace from gossip and speculation, taking everything very much in his stride, approaching everyone as he found them – well, in most cases.

'You're devilish quiet, Andy,' opined McKirdy.

'I daresay. I've been pondering on much we've heard tonight from Munro here. It's brought some stories to mind. Aye, tales I'd forgotten all about – fae years back.'

Peeny looked at McKirdy, raising his eyes to the ceiling. For everyone knew – as much as they respected the man – that once Duncan embarked upon a yarn, great swathes of your life were likely to be eaten away. 'You'll need to be quick wae your story, Andy,' said Peeny. 'Hoynes or no Hoynes, we'll have to head for the stones soon to make midnight.'

'Always in a hurry, Peeny. You should slow down and smell the fish for a change.' He shifted in his chair, still staring into the flames of the fire. 'When I was a lad, I mind my faither telling me o' one night just like this. It was the Auld New Year – och, must be o'er seven decades ago.'

McKirdy leaned into Peeny's ear. 'It'll take him another seventy years tae tell the tale.'

'I can hear you, McKirdy,' said Andy Duncan. 'My eyes might no' be what they once were, but there's bugger-all wrong wae my lugs.' He coughed, indicating the story was to resume. 'This place, the auld village in which we find ourselves, has long since been abandoned. But it stood for hundreds o' years, right back to the times o' the Vikings. The very stones we're making for shortly were held in high esteem by the Northmen. So much so, that they wouldn't think o' embarkation on any kind o' caper before they left some silver at them. We don't have an abundance o' the silver, but we still toast them wae good whisky, and that's much the same thing.'

'I'd rather have a dram than silver,' said McMichael.

'Then you're a bigger fool than I took you for, Jimmy. For you can purchase a fair cargo o' whisky wae silver, but you'll get damn-all silver for a bottle o' the good stuff, and that's a fact.'

Suitably chastised, McMichael found nothing more to say.

'Now, back in my father's time, they were all gathered here as we are now. Mind you, the bothy hadn't been raised then, so they slept under canvas amongst the ruins.' He took a sip of whisky. 'This night, they were making their wae doon fae the stones, having partaken in the usual ceremonies.'

'Aye, drinking a bucketful,' said Peeny.

'The observances that we still follow to this day,' retorted Duncan sharply, somewhat piqued by yet another interruption to his story. 'Anyhow, they spied something on their way doon the wee path. It was a boat, but nothing like what was to be found at that time. Ach, my father had notions fae time to time. But he described it, and hearing Munro this night has brought the memory back to mind. Long, sleek, wae fire blazing fore and aft – just as you say.' He raised his glass to Munro. 'The theory was at the time that each Auld New Year the spirits o' the Northmen made for the stones to pay their respects.'

'See, I'm no' wrong in the heid,' said Munro.

'They canna have been much good at telling time,' said Malcolm Connelly.

'How so?' asked Duncan.

'Well, if oor boys had been up at the stones to take in the Auld New Year, the spirits o' the Vikings doon in the bay must have missed the boat – if you pardon the pun.'

'You're a right pedant, Malcolm,' said Andy Duncan. 'It's a trait I've noted in you long before now. You'll understand that the men from the north weren't in possession o' wristwatches and the like that we have now. They held their time by the moon and the stars, and such a thing isna accurate to the very second. Nor does it matter, for oor time has little consequence in the great scheme o' things.'

'We're surrounded by ghostly Vikings, then – is that what you're telling us, Andy?' said Peeny.

'This was their settlement; they founded this wee place. So I don't see why their memory o' them widna be abundant. Anyway, there's more to the story.'

'For any's sake, it's a bloody saga,' McKirdy whispered to Peeny.

'Wheesht, McKirdy, for this is the best bit.' Andy sat forward in his chair, his eyes now averted from the fire, as he glanced at them all, one by one. 'There was one Archibald MacEachran – a fine fisherman, by all accounts – in the party. As we all know, there's no' an older family in this peninsula than the MacEachrans – they were here long before the Norse arrived. Some say they became bitter enemies.'

This statement was met with nods of general agreement, it being well known that the MacEachrans were descended from 'the people of the horse' who had first inhabited Kintyre. 'I'm no' so fond o' them myself,' said Peeny. 'Right thrawn buggers, the lot o' them.'

Duncan continued unabashed, as a log spat loudly in the fireplace. 'Though they were all a bit put off by the vision in the bay, MacEachran was near demented. No doubt, his blood calling to him doon the generations, fair warning the man o' the danger o' the wild men fae the North.' Duncan paused, his wrinkled face drawn into a grimace, rheumy eyes narrowed. 'All they wanted was to be back at their camp, safe and sound wae a warming dram in their hands. But with their encampment in sight – the very ground on which we find ourselves this night – a terrible thing happened.' Andy Duncan's voice was little more than a whisper now. 'MacEachran's legs were suddenly fair rooted to the spot wae fright. Suddenly, out of nowhere, there was this mighty crack!' He made an expansive gesture with his arms. As he did so, the door swung open on its hinges, making Peeny shriek and jump from his chair, tipping a bottle of whisky to the earthen floor, where its contents glugged out until McKirdy dived to rescue what was left. As though delayed by the shock, young Danny let out a blood-curdling yell, as Andy Duncan, the storyteller himself, clasped a hand to his chest, his old heart having leapt with fright.

'Man, but yous are right jumpy,' said Hoynes, framed in the doorway, a wisp of fog trailing into the bothy from the cold night behind him.

18

The chase had taken the Customs men almost the full length of the Isle of Arran. The flickering light that looked so much like flame had always been just within sight, but just out of reach. Despite Marshall's encouragement, they seemed unable to make any ground on the vessel they assumed to be the *Girl Maggie*.

'What on earth does Hoynes have for engines? The boat's jet-propelled!' exclaimed the frustrated collector.

Cummings stroked his chin. He'd been at sea long enough to recognise the knot presently in his stomach was the intimation of an instinct that all was not well. 'It's the fire I don't understand, sir.'

'The man's clearly using it to trick us. Any sensible mariner would be showing lights fore and aft in these conditions. If Hoynes thinks he's put us off the scent by the use of fire, he's got another think coming.' He stared at the flames shimmering in the fog ahead. 'Surely we can get more from the engine? This vessel is designed to overtake lesser craft and bring them to book.'

'We're at full speed, sir. I'm as puzzled as you that we can't make any headway.'

To his right through the mist, Marshall saw lights. 'Is that Lochranza, Cummings?'

'Yes, sir. We'll soon be out in the firth. With a bit of luck, once we're past the island, this will clear and we'll be able to get a better fix on Hoynes.'

'Good. Damn the man. I don't know how he thinks he can continue to outrun us.'

'It has to be said, he's done no' too bad so far, sir.'

Marshall picked up the radio mouthpiece from its cradle. 'Her Majesty's Revenue cutter *Diane* to Clyde Coastguard. Come in, over.' As he waited for a reply he turned to Marshall. 'I'm determined to catch this rascal. We'll have another vessel head him off in the firth – the Royal Navy, if necessary. We'll cut him off!'

As Marshall called for assistance over the radio, Cummings noted the lights of Lochranza were now behind them. As he stared out, he fancied he could see the mist begin to thin as they headed for the narrow channel between Firdale and the last stretch of the Isle of Arran. 'Sir, I think I was right. The conditions seem to be improving.'

Marshall hung the mouthpiece back on its cradle. 'Let the fox see the chicken, eh? Good stuff!'

But, to the dismay of both men on the bridge, as the mist cleared to reveal again the stars under which they'd begun their journey, so any sign of the flames they'd been following all the way up the sound had disappeared.

'He's vanished, sir!' said Cummings, his mouth gaping open.

'He can't have done. I'll get a man on the searchlight. He's likely extinguished the fire when he saw the mist clear. Hoynes can't be far away.'

As Marshall ran off to supervise the searchlight, Cummings remained unconvinced. Though the moon was no more than a crescent, the night was bright with stars. From the dimly lit bridge, he could see their reflection in the dark water of the Firth of Clyde. What he couldn't see was any sign of a vessel, fire or no fire. His hands gripped the ship's wheel. 'We were following something tonight,' he muttered to himself under his breath. 'But I'm not sure it was Sandy Hoynes.'

Hamish was on his third bumper of whisky before they were all ready to head up to the stones. His skipper took him in with a leery eye.

'Man, but you've got a fair drouth the night, Hamish. We've plenty whisky to go round – don't worry. You don't have to drink it all at once.'

Hamish looked back at him with a heavy-lidded gaze. 'Sandy, I'll no' lie to you. I got a right scare tonight.' His voice was already slurred. 'I could picture me an' you standing in the dock o' the High Court in Glasgow and being dragged off to the jail. Aye, where we'd spend years.'

'Don't be daft, Hamish. There was no risk o' that. I reckon it was some prankster fae Firdale at work. You know fine what buggers they are for a wind-up, eh?' Hoynes puffed on a pipe, a spare one borrowed from Andy Duncan, his own still somewhere on the *Girl Maggie*'s wheelhouse floor. 'Besides, we'd have been tried in the Sherriff Court in Kinloch. It's no' as though we murdered anyone.'

'Och, that's a weight off my mind, Sandy,' said Hamish. 'I'm no' sure what I was worrying about at all.'

'Sarcasm isna your strong suit, son,' said Hoynes. 'I had the entire matter in hand start to finish. You saw yourself how slick the operation was wae thon raft. Man, it was like the Marine Commandos during the war. We could have stormed Greece wae such fine organisation.'

'But the Commandos weren't smuggling whisky, they were fighting Hitler. There's a big difference when you think aboot it, Sandy.'

'Who said anything aboot smuggling? We were just helping oot some dry-mouthed souls. A mission o' mercy, nothing more.'

'Whisky in old lemonade bottles. Do you think I sailed up the Clyde in a banana boat?'

'You're a right mistrustful bugger, Hamish. Aye, and insulting with it. As though I'd be up to any such caper. I've a good mind to inform your mother o' your suspicious state o' mind when we get back to Kinloch. Sheer paranoia, and that's a fact.' He lowered his voice. 'And I'll thank you no' to be making any more mention of tonight's goings-on. You know fine what a band o' auld fishwives this team are. Before you know it, we'll be the Bonnie and Clyde of Kinloch, once they start at the gossip.'

'Who are Bonnie and Clyde, Sandy?'

'A right pair o' scunners fae America. Robbers and thieves. Though if the comparison was made, I'd have tae be Bonnie, because you're no' blessed wae good looks.'

'Eh?' Hamish looked abashed.

'They funny eyes you've got – aye, and the way your hair is on the retreat. You're an oil painting, but one o' little merit.'

Hamish leaned into his skipper with a stagger. 'And what happened wae those flames, tell me that?'

Hoynes coughed. 'Flames? I'm sure I've no idea what you're on aboot!'

'I know fine you saw them, Sandy. They flashed between us and the Customs cutter. We're only at liberty because they took off after them, and you know it!'

Hoynes took another puff. 'If I was you, I'd lay off the drink. I'm sure your brain is fair addled wae it, and you no mair than a youngster.' He shook his head, but there was something about his expression that rendered this statement unconvincing.

'Come on!' shouted Peeny. 'We'll miss midnight if we're no' careful.'

One by one, the Kinloch fishermen left the warmth of the bothy and stepped out into the freezing night. Frost sparkled on the branches of the fir trees as they plodded along a narrow path in single file. There was no mist now, and the clean, fresh smell of pine was strong in the air, mixing with the tang of the restless sea far below, where the *Girl Maggie* nestled safely in the tiny cove.

Hamish and his skipper were bringing up the rear, just behind Andy Duncan – who, for his age, had a healthy stride. He stopped for a moment and beckoned Hoynes.

'A wee word, Sandy.'

Hoynes approached the older man. 'Aye, what can I help you wae, Andy?'

'I've been remembering times past, Sandy. And I should tell you that I've a right sore feeling in my heart.'

'A sore feeling? Should we call the Firdale doctor?'

Duncan stared at Hoynes, a man almost twenty years his junior. 'I'm thinking you know full well what I mean.' He turned on his heel and followed the others towards the old stones.

✧

Now out in the broad firth, with searchlight deployed, it soon became obvious to Marshall that, somehow, Hoynes had given them the slip. He bounded back onto the bridge, his mood dark.

'This is damnable, Cummings, just damnable. The man's like a ghost.'

Cummings bowed his head.

'What on earth is the matter with you?'

'Och, nothing, sir. Just auld tales and ancient fancies. Men o' the sea like myself are prone to different ideas at times like these.'

'Such as?' replied Marshall impatiently.

'Nothing in particular. But rogues of all generations are thought to look after their own – no matter how many years have intervened.'

'Good grief, Cummings. Don't tell me you seriously thought we were following a ghost ship. I must say, this nonsense does you little credit.'

Cummings merely shrugged and looked out at distant lights on the shores of the Firth of Clyde.

'Hoynes is holed up in some bay. Arran is dotted with them. Your job is to know these waters as well as he does!'

'And that I do, sir.'

'So, your explanation is that he was rescued by some spectre dedicated to the liberty of every smuggler and rogue to be found? A kind of patron saint of thieves.'

'All I'll say is that I've seen my fair share of strange things at sea, sir.'

'I'm here to prove you wrong, man. We'll double back and run the coast of Arran close – examine every nook and cranny

104

under the searchlight. I tell you, once Hoynes sees we're dedicated to the task, he'll have no choice other than to break for cover. My guess is, just before dawn. He won't want to be pursued in broad daylight. He won't be able to pull any of his little tricks.'

'If you say so, sir.'

'Yes, I damn well do. Get a grip, Cummings, and turn us back towards Arran.'

'Aye, aye, sir.' Grimly, the first mate turned the big wheel, and soon the *Diane* was sailing as close to the coast of the island as she could, a powerful searchlight probing every rocky beach and tiny inlet.

19

Hoynes stopped and leaned against a stout oak tree. A life at sea didn't prepare you for the rigours of traversing the land. While the skipper was more than happy to scale any mountainous wave behind the wheel of his fishing boat, he wasn't quite so comfortable on foot facing a climb. He patted his belly and took a deep breath.

'You're out of condition,' said Hamish. The cold night air appeared to have cleared his head, and he looked much less tired and emotional.

'Wae one thing and another, it's been a busy few days. You remember, I'm more than twice your age, Hamish. Though I'll be long dead, remember these words when you're in your sixties. It's a hellish thing, but, damn me, nothing works the way it once did, and that's a fact. Man, that's why I'm telling you to get a move on in the marriage stakes. There's nothing worse than a man who likes sitting by the fire wae a good dram and the newspaper married to a younger woman keen to be about the jolly old thing of an evening.'

'The "jolly old thing"?'

'Don't tell me I have to teach you aboot the birds and bees, too? I signed up for getting your navigating and fishing skills up to muster, no' matters o' an intimate nature.'

Hamish looked puzzled for a few moments, then what his skipper was saying dawned on him. 'Here, Sandy, there's no need for that. I'm perfectly aware o' my duties in that department – aye, an' more than capable o' their execution, I'll have you know.' Despite the cargo of whisky he'd consumed, the whole subject was enough to make him blush but he had to defend himself.

'Well, I'm heartily glad o' it. All you need to get on wae now is putting theory into practice. I'd a picture in my mind there o' me fairly having to lead you to the marital bed, a bit like the auld kings.'

'The auld kings? What capers were they up to?'

'There was no privacy in that job, man. You'd to get on wae it in full view o' the court. Imagine! A whole room full o' folk keeping you right at every turn, eh?'

Hamish shuddered. Though he wasn't prepared to admit it, the whole idea of an intimate interaction with a member of the opposite sex made him rather nervous. The very thought of having to share such activity under the scrutiny of his elders and betters was unimaginable.

As though he'd read his young charge's mind, Hoynes piped up. 'I know what you're thinking, Hamish. You're fair visualising Peeny and McKirdy standing over you in the throes o' passion, handing out helpful hints and tips, eh?'

'I was thinking nothing o' the kind, Sandy.'

'I widna worry too much aboot auld Andy Duncan. He's probably forgotten anything he knew aboot such things. I'm sure he'd be happier wae a good bowl o' soup than any cavorting. Come to think o' it, so would I – as long as it was a decent broth, mind you. I canna bear a weak, watery offering.'

'Can we change the subject, Sandy?'

'Of course. I was just making sure you were acquainted wae your duties as the man o' the house. It's good to know you've at least got some notion.'

'Have you drawn enough breath? We'll need to catch up with the rest.'

'There's plenty time, and in any case, we've no' far to go.'

The skipper and first mate of the *Girl Maggie* continued their slog up the winding path as an owl hooted plaintively in the woods beyond.

In a few more minutes, the path broadened out, and Hamish saw the rest of the party gathered in a small clearing, their oil lamps illuminating the scene with a warm, almost ethereal glow.

As he and Hoynes approached, Hamish could see two little stones. They were of an unusual shape – one like an oversized mushroom with a dimpled top, the other a more geometric shape, akin to a triangle. Though the latter was the bigger, neither of the tiny monuments were above knee height.

'Ah, there we are, the Auld Man and Woman – the Couple,' said Hoynes, a beatific smile spreading across his bearded face.

'They're no' exactly what I was expecting,' said Hamish.

Hoynes looked at him through narrowed eyes. 'Exactly what *were* you expecting? The Hanging Gardens o' Babylon? Stonehenge?'

'Maybe something bigger – a bit more dramatic?'

Hoynes shook his head. 'As you'll no doubt find out, size is of no consequence. These stones are older than you can even comprehend. Aye, and they have a power that is hard to explain.'

Hamish gazed at the Auld Man and Woman under the lamplight, then at his companions, who were all contemplating the stones with great reverence.

'Here,' said Peeny. 'There's something glistening on the auld fella.'

'Andy?' Danny blurted.

'Just you watch yoursel', son,' said Andy Duncan.

'No. Look.' Peeny bent over and picked an object from the smaller stone, which he examined at close quarters under the flickering light of his oil lamp. 'Damn me, I think it might be gold!'

Hoynes shouldered his way through to where Peeny was standing – the very mention of gold a magnet for his attention – and snatched the item from his companion's grasp. The object was only a few inches long, and though he'd suspected Peeny's gold was that of a fool, he soon realised his old friend was right. The thing shone in the dim light with a buttery glow that could only be that of the precious metal. Geometric shapes carved along its length looked like coiled snakes.

'Don't you have any ideas aboot pocketing that, Sandy,' said Peeny, aggrieved he'd been dispossessed of the item in such a brusque manner.

'It's a gold brooch,' declared Hoynes. He took in the swirling artistry engraved on the tiny piece of jewellery with wide eyes.

'Looks like it was only made yesterday,' said Peeny.

'That it does,' agreed Andy Duncan, now beside Hoynes and peering at the golden brooch through thick reading glasses. 'It's a right bonnie thing, so it is.'

The rest of the party huddled round, anxious to have a look at the curiosity.

'Must have been left by one of the Firdale boys. What do you think, Munro?' asked McKirdy.

'You must be doing better at the fishing in Kinloch than we are in Firdale. There's no' much gold to be had in oor village. And what there is stays firmly round the fingers o' married women.' Munro folded his arms in adamant dismissiveness.

Hoynes looked mesmerised. 'I've seen the like o' this before,' he said dreamily.

'Whereabouts? No' in the window o' Blue's jewellers in Kinloch, that's for sure. The man sells cheap tat,' said Malcolm Connelly.

'No, not at all.' Hoynes held the brooch in cupped hands to give every man a better view. 'I saw it in a book about the Vikings. I'd bet anything it's their work.'

'You'll be finished wae the fishing and getting a job at the British Museum then,' said Peeny sarcastically.

'Ow!' exclaimed Hoynes suddenly. He dropped the brooch like a hot coal.

'What on earth's wrong?' asked McKirdy.

'The damn thing burned me!' Hoynes blew on each hand to ease the pain.

'Your backside,' said Peeny. 'You should be on the stage, Sandy. Drama is never far off when you're around.' He bent forward and picked the brooch off the ground. 'See, not a problem, as cool as a cucumber . . . oh, you bugger!' He exclaimed as he, too, dropped the brooch and rubbed his hands with a grimace. 'You were right, Sandy. Hot as a fresh fish supper!'

They all regarded the golden object, now lying on the pine needles that covered the ground.

'Put it back on the stone!' said Andy Duncan in a commanding voice. 'That's where it was placed, and that's where it belongs.'

'Do it yourself. I'm no' burning my hands again,' said Peeny.

The old man knelt stiffly over the brooch, picked it up, and placed it carefully back in the bowl-like indentation on the stone. 'There, that's order restored. Now, let's be about our business, for the auld year is about to turn.'

20

Hamish was glad to have consumed a few drams as the old members of the party droned on with their toasts and mysterious incantations – mutterings that made little sense to him. He had been expecting something more raucous, more entertaining. Frankly, this was a disappointment.

He turned to young Danny. 'I was hoping for mair than this, eh?'

'You've to listen to what they're at, Hamish. My father says that we'll have to do this one day, and we should take note. He'd be up here himself if it wasn't for his hip.'

Hamish looked less than impressed by this point of view. He watched Andy Duncan, who appeared to be taking the lead in proceedings. 'Is he at the Gaelic?'

'I'm no' sure,' said Danny. 'I canna understand a word o' it, to be honest.'

'We'll have a job remembering all this for when oor time comes, eh? I hope somebody has it all written down.' He shuffled from foot to foot uncomfortably. 'Here, will you hold my glass, nature is taking its course on my bladder. I'll nip into these trees for some relief.'

Handing his dram to his companion, Hamish made for the shelter of the fir trees. He reckoned that having a pee at such a sombre ceremony may be considered bad form, so he made sure he walked far enough into the forest so that he was well out of sight.

Though it was dark, and he could hear the sound of small creatures rustling through the woods, he carried on. Thankfully, the soothing balm of whisky had insulated him from the nerves he'd normally have experienced under such circumstances. He pressed on until he found a tree far enough away to be discreet. Hamish breathed a sigh as he relieved himself against the trunk. It was a damnable facet of enjoying a drink. The more you consumed, the more often you had to go.

The deed done, he was about to make his way back to the stones, when something caught his eye. Through the trees shone a light, green then red, seemingly swirling between the tall pines. Intrigued, Hamish made his way towards it.

One by one, each man pulled a half-bottle of whisky from his bag and poured it over the taller of the two stones. In the bowl of the other, on top of the gold brooch, they placed a coin.

Andy Duncan looked at Peeny with distaste as he laid down a ha'penny. 'Man, is that all you can manage? It's an insult to the auld fella, right enough.'

'I've a son still at home, if you remember. He was laid off by Martin the joiner last year, so every penny counts. It's the gesture that makes the difference, no' the sum, Andy.'

'If you say so.'

'Before the war we used to pour out a bottle, now it's a half-bottle. It's the same thing.'

'Rationing put a stop to that, Peeny. And besides, wae the price o' drink now, what wae taxes and all, I'm sure the stones are happy wae what they're given – adjusted for inflation, as they say on the wireless.'

'Good, so the same goes for currency.' Peeny smiled, happy that he'd made his point.

Young Danny made his way to the stones. With great reverence, he poured his whisky over the Auld Woman and placed a shilling in the bowl of the Auld Man.

'That's the spirit,' said Andy Duncan. 'No lack o' respect and generosity, son. It makes my heart glad.' Purposefully, he stared at Peeny.

'My faither says it's best to give what you can. The stones did him proud during his time at the fishing. He'll no' forget it, he says.'

'A grand sentiment, right enough. Your father was always a generous man – something that can't be said for every fisherman, sadly.' Andy Duncan shook his head.

Before Peeny could protest, Hoynes looked round the small party. 'Has anyone seen Hamish?'

'He left me his dram and telt me he was off for a pee, Mr Hoynes,' said Danny.

'When was this?'

'Och, a while now, come to think of it.'

It was Hoynes's turn to shake his head. 'He'll likely be lost amongst the trees. I better go and look for him. Young folk these days . . . Which way did he go?'

'Danny pointed to a break in the trees behind them.

'He can't have got far. I'll no' be long, gentlemen.'

Hoynes grabbed a rusty oil lamp and went in search of his first mate, quietly cursing as he did so.

For a while, the swirling red and green lights were elusive. But eventually, Hamish happened upon a clearing in the trees, just ahead of a point where the hill fell away. He looked to the sky in wonder. Curtains of red and green light were floating in the starry sky, changing shape and form in a mesmerising way. He'd heard tales of the Northern Lights, but apart from a green glow above Jura late one evening, he hadn't seen them – certainly not like this.

Hamish was so impressed that he decided to take a seat on the ground and study the whole phenomenon more closely. The lights in the sky were reflected in the waters of the sound, making the whole place look magical – enchanted – like a child's fairy tale. He'd been told that the Aurora Borealis was a common sight further to the north. But tonight Kintyre was being treated to the full display, as the sky above swirled and shimmered with vibrant colour.

For emergencies, he'd stashed away a hip flask of whisky in his pocket. He gulped down a dram, eyes still on the spectacle. Old fishermen chanting incantations over two wee stones was nothing compared to this.

For the first time on the trip, Hamish was glad he'd come along.

I hope Sandy's spied this, he thought to himself.

Hoynes was now lost in a forest of thick, tall pines. Though the oil lamp afforded a little light in his immediate vicinity, it did nothing to aid a wider perspective. He looked above, noting no stars in the sky, and reckoned this was because the thick canopy of branches above him was obscuring any celestial light.

'Damn me, Hamish,' he swore to himself. 'I'll wring your neck when I find you.'

He stopped for a moment and considered his predicament. If he was to go on, he was sure to become hopelessly lost. In any case, he was sure even Hamish, dizzy as he was at times, wouldn't have trekked so far away from the stones just to answer the call of nature.

He turned on his heel and began to make his way back the way he was sure he'd come.

'Hamish!' he shouted at the top of his voice. But so dense was the forest, his voice seemed strangely muted –as though he was calling from under a thick blanket.

'Bugger!' he cursed again. 'You're for your jotters when we get back to Kinloch.'

Then, to his great dismay, the flame in his oil lamp began to gutter and fade. He turned the knob on the side of the lamp desperately, but nothing happened. However, touching its base, Hoynes noticed his hand was wet. The old lamp had been leaking oil. Slowly, despite his best efforts, the flame flickered once more and died.

Now he was in complete darkness.

21

Marshall had travelled the whole length of Arran, checking every nook and cranny with the cutter's powerful searchlight. They'd found nothing, apart from a young courting couple who had braved the cold night for the purposes of getting to know each other better in an old ketch. The pair looked shocked when they were illuminated by *Diane*'s bright beam. However, Cummings managed to quell their embarrassment with a quick chat about the weather and the offer of a packet of Woodbines.

'That's us by the King's Caves, sir. It looks as though Hoynes must have taken off somewhere else.' Cummings looked to his boss for further instructions.

Collector Marshall was busy staring at the sky. 'A wonderful display tonight, eh?'

'Aye, it is. I'd welcome the lights on most nights, but not so much on this one.'

'Why so?'

'Auld tales o' nonsense, I daresay. But they used to reckon that if the lights shone at Auld New Year, the laws o' nature somehow meant nothing. The dead and the living shared the same place. But you're no' a fan o' such fancies, are you, Mr Marshall.'

'Indeed I am not. I'm more a fan of catching miscreants. But, most regrettably, I think we've let one give us the slip this evening.' Thankfully, Marshall's righteous zeal had ebbed away the further down Arran's coast they had patrolled and the less likely it seemed that Hoynes was to be found. 'You don't think he made it round to the other side of the island without us noticing, do you?'

'He'd have to have had six engines to accomplish that, sir. From what I'm told, the one they have on the *Girl Maggie* isn't an up-to-date model. In fact, I'd go so far as to say that it's well past its best.'

'I just don't know.' Marshall thought back to the call he'd had the previous morning. It was after midnight now, and he'd been on the go without a break for far too long. Now that the adrenaline of the chase had dissipated, his eyes felt heavy, and he wanted nothing more than to get his head down for a few hours.

Spotting this, his first mate felt it appropriate to make a suggestion. 'Why don't you go to the cabin for a wee nap, sir? I can handle things up here. I've one notion o' a place we've no' explored.'

'Where's that?'

'A part o' the coast I heard about a long time ago when I was at the fishing. Back on the Kintyre side. They call it the Smuggler's Hole.'

'Now that's bloody appropriate. If Hoynes is anywhere, it'll be in that place. Though, for the life of me, I can't work out how he could have made it back to Kintyre with us hot on his heels.'

'These auld skippers are up to all sorts of tricks, sir. I wouldn't put anything past the man. You get below, and I'll be sure and wake you if we come up with anything.'

Yawning noisily, Marshall made his way from the bridge to seek the sanctuary of a short sleep and a break from thoughts of Sandy Hoynes.

Though Sandy Hoynes wasn't a man prone to unmerited fear, he had to admit that being without a light, deep in a thick forest of trees and in a heavy frost, was something that left him rather unsettled. Not only that, he had lost all sense of direction and was worried that he'd become even more lost if he went in just about any direction.

Hoynes decided that the best course of action was to make for a gap in the pines, where at least he might be afforded a glimpse of the sky and some kind of orientation via the stars, with which he was well acquainted.

He moved slowly forward, hands held out before him, helping his navigation from tree to tree. The going was slow and hard, and his spirits were low. The enticing smell of pine resin was now overpowering, making his eyes water. His mouth – following a few whiskies – was dry. All told, he was as miserable as sin. A night of tales, drinking and old traditions ruined by his accident-prone first mate. He made a mental note to have Hamish paint the whole vessel when they returned to Kinloch. But a little voice in his head piped up with, 'If you make it back to Kinloch.'

After about twenty minutes of stumbling around in the dark, he decided to rest up. He eased his back down against a stout tree trunk and, shivering with cold, sighed deeply at his plight.

Meanwhile, with the Northern Lights having faded to little more than a fluorescent glow in the sky, their spell over Hamish weakened. He wasn't sure how long he'd been staring at the celestial display, but whatever time it was, he supposed that it was too long.

He stood up, turning his back on the sound and assessed the forest of trees through which he had come. Hamish stroked his chin, trying to decide by which route he'd arrived at this place. To aid this process, he took the flask from his pocket and took another draw of the whisky.

'I think that looks right,' he said to himself, squinting at a narrow path that disappeared into the trees.

Glad to be on the move, and buoyed by the spirit, he whistled a jaunty reel as he took off to find his companions.

⬩✧⬩

Back at the stones, Andy Duncan was less than happy. Even the warmth of the whisky he'd consumed wasn't enough to keep the cold from making his old bones ache.

'We can only assume they've made their way back to bothy. Aye, and it's time we did likewise.'

There were general mutterings of agreement, for each of them was cold and wanted nothing more than to be by the warming fire of their temporary home for the night. Only young Danny demurred. 'They'll find it hard to survive the night in this cold, will they no'?'

McKirdy blew on his hands. 'None of us will survive if we don't get back into the warmth soon. Look at auld Andy. His face is blue. I swear I can see it fae here.'

'Can't we get help?' Danny was a thoughtful lad, having been brought up to look out for others by his fisherman father.

'What do you suggest? The RNLI?' Peeny sneered. 'They'll no' come trooping all the way up here. It's the sea for them, and I'm sure they've no forestry equivalent.'

'Sandy will turn up. A man like that has infinite wiles at his disposal,' said Malcolm Connelly. 'Man, he and Hamish are likely sitting by the fire in the bothy right now, wondering what's up wae us.'

'Right. So we head back,' said Andy Duncan through the chatter of his teeth.

They decision was made. With their oil lamps lighting the way, the party of fishermen headed away from the stones and back down the path, minus two of their number.

Danny caught up with Jim McMichael. 'What if the same thing that happened to thon MacEachran has befallen Mr Hoynes and Hamish?

'Don't be daft, son. That's just a story. They'll be fine, you'll see. I've known Hoynes since I was a wean. It'll take more than a few trees and a cold night to do for him, let me assure you.'

All the same, Danny bit his lip in concern as they progressed down the hill, losing sight of the Auld Stones.

22

Collector Marshall's Dream

The gentle sway of the cutter lulled Marshall to sleep. He was stretched out along a bench seat in the small cabin below deck. As he drifted off, the irritation at not apprehending Sandy Hoynes was replaced by the muddled fancies of the world of dreams and the subconscious.

He was back on the bridge, alone, peering out into an impenetrable fog. Though no light could be seen, the intermittent drone of a fog horn could be heard, its lowing tone like some great beast lost in the darkness, warning wayward mariners off the rocks and skerries.

The vessel appeared out of the fog like a wraith. Though this craft had fine lines and looked of masterful build, it was ruined. The square sail, striped with red and white, was tattered and burned. It hung loosely in the dead calm. At the prow, a carved likeness of a snake was hanging, broken at its base. Sinews of pale, newly exposed wood cracked and creaked. A great gash in the hull was fortunately just above the waterline, though any persistent sea would surely sink her very quickly.

Fore and aft, tall braziers stood on stout poles. The fire that once blazed from them was now nothing but dying embers.

Wisps of fog clung to them like the thin fingers of a spirit intent upon pulling this fine craft into the other world, the dominion of death.

Along her side was a broken cluster of targes – round shields, split and broken, their centre bosses battered – the tattered remnants of defeat, trophies of failure.

For Marshall, the whole scene spoke of pride and power brought low, as the great buildings of the ancients were now nothing but ruins in shifting desert sands. The stench of death hung about this ghost ship like a curse.

He could see a man hanging over the side, long blond hair trailing into the water. Even in the dim light, the gash on his arm was black and livid, another on his shoulder deeper, almost severing the limb from his torso. Beside him, another man lay back at an impossible angle, a wicked sword piercing his neck from back to front, pinning him to the mast behind. His arms were spread out wide in death, as though he was imploring those who might have the power to do such things to bring him back to the life he loved.

Marshall wanted to scream, but no sound would come. He pulled at the wheel, anxious not to collide with this vision of hell and destruction. But the ruined boat seemed only to drift closer and closer.

He heard movement from behind and turned to call his first mate to his side. But the man who faced him wasn't Cummings. This dark-clad figure shimmered as though his body wasn't quite corporeal. Despite this, the black blood that ran down his face and the split in his skull looked all too real. Still, there was about him a glimmer of light, a flickering symbol of fading life.

The apparition stared at Marshall, flaxen hair streaked dark by gore. 'Why are you here?' The big man's voice was slow and accented, but Marshall could understand him well enough.

'It's you that shouldn't be here,' Marshall stammered.

The tall man bowed his head, his arms hanging loose at his side. Marshall noticed that one of his hands was missing; only the stump remained, dripping blood onto the wooden decking of the bridge. 'Then we are already passing into another realm. This is the Thin Place.' The voice was no more than a whisper, but in it was the loss of all hope. No despair, just the resignation of defeat, the surrender to the inevitable.

'Can I help you?' Marshall didn't know why he asked the question but felt compelled to do so; whether out of compassion or fear, he wasn't sure.

Black leather creaked as the apparition before him raised his head. His eyes were a piercing blue, his gaze so penetrating that Marshall held up a hand to shield his own eyes, fearing this man was looking into his soul.

'You and I are on a journey. Our paths have crossed, that is all. You find me as you find me. My journey is near its end, so I fear yours may be too. It's the only way I can explain us being together at this moment in time. Unless . . .'

Marshall gasped for air, as though he was being slowly strangled. 'I don't understand what you mean – unless what?'

His visitor laughed weakly. 'We all try to escape the end. I am lucky – I see mine coming. You, I think, do not see yours. But that is the way of things. There is nothing to fear, for nothing truly comes to an end. Life is only how we see ourselves at one point in time. There are many lives.'

He pointed a finger at Marshall. 'I have known you before, as you have known me. We will meet again, but we will never be on the same side. We will never be brothers, always enemies. Though there is more that binds us than mere enmity.'

'What – what binds us?' Marshall couldn't understand why he felt compelled to ask the things he did, but he uttered the words nonetheless.

'Eternity – eternity binds us for ever. You on one side, me on the other.'

'I've never seen you before, so how can we be bound by this *eternity*?'

'By a moment in time – by this moment – by every moment. We are of different worlds now, but those worlds are only separated by a whisper. They collide in places like this, and always do so for a reason.'

The image of the man before him was fading.

'See not only what is before you, but what lies behind and is yet to come.'

'You're talking in riddles!'

'Listen to the blood that flows through you. Because it has flowed for ever.' With that, the man disappeared like a clearing mist.

Marshall turned back to the wheel. Both vessels were about to collide. He fell to the floor and braced for the impact.

This time the scream came.

23

Hamish could smell smoke. He halted his progress through the trees and sniffed at the air like a dog. He was sure it came from the direction he'd been walking. The thought that the cosy little bothy may be nearby cheered him. His passage from the hill from which he'd watched the Northern Lights to this point had been a happy meander, whistling his favourite tunes and thinking on happy times past.

Hamish weaved his way between the pines. Then, sure enough, the trees began to thin and he found himself atop a little outcrop. Not far below, the bothy was picked out under the stars.

Hamish paused at the door and took a deep breath. The aroma of peat smoke and whisky was in the air, intermingled with pine resin and the tang of the sea. He was worried about his skipper, and how angry he'd be that his first mate had missed much of the ceremony at the Auld Stones. Being the polite man his mother had brought him up to be, he knocked on the door before throwing it open.

But the scene inside the bothy wasn't at all what he'd expected. All of the familiar faces looked grim, and all were directed at him.

'Where on earth have you been?' asked Andy Duncan, perched on a chair by the fire alongside Munro of Firdale.

'Och, I had to answer a call o' nature, but, damn me, did I no' get lost. But looking on the brighter side, I got a rare glimpse o' the Northern Lights. Just fair amazing, they were. The whole sky was dancing wae red and green. Like great curtains, it was. Just as I've heard them described. It made my night, and no mistake.' Hamish looked around for some appreciation of his tale, but there was none. Indeed, if anything, his companions bore even more disapproving expressions than they had when he'd first arrived.

'Well, I'm glad you had a good time,' said Peeny, staring at the floor.

'I'm right sorry to have missed the tribute to the stones. I know how much store yous all place upon it. But a man canna help getting lost, and that's just the fact o' it. Anyway, I'm back safe and sound, and there's bound to be many other years to be at this caper.' For the first time since entering the bothy, Hamish sensed that something was wrong. And whatever this something was, it wasn't just the matter of his missing the ceremony at the stones. 'Here, where's Sandy?' he asked, looking about the small space for his skipper.

'Man, you're quick off the mark, Hamish, eh? There you are, blethering on about lights in the sky, when all the time your skipper is missing, and only the good Lord knows where. Lost he is, off looking for you.' Andy Duncan shook his head.

'All this wae the Northern Lights. Have you been on they drugs?' Malcolm Connelly said. 'It's only a matter o' days since you were banging on aboot free love and that. I can only wonder at what your poor mother thinks of such capers.'

'But . . . where can he be?' Hamish stammered.

'Man, if we knew that, don't you think we'd be off and found him?' said Munro.

'You know this place, Mr Munro. Surely we can have a scout about and get a bearing on him?' Hamish looked desperate.

'I'm fae Firdale, that much is true. But you surely don't think I'm acquainted wae every tree and shrub in the place? Do you know much about the woodland around Kinloch? In any event, I'm a fisherman, no' a forest elf. Aye, and in case you've no' noticed, it's pitch-black outside, and damn well freezing into the bargain.'

'No man can last long in such conditions,' opined Jim McMichael. 'It's nothing short o' a miracle you made it back yourself.'

'We can't just sit here and do nothing!' wailed Hamish at the top of his voice.

'If there's no sign o' him at first light we'll fan out and search,' said Andy Duncan, clearly the self-appointed leader of the group due to his great age and the respect in which he was held. 'But I fear it's a corpse we're likely to find. There's no' a mair resourceful body than Sandy Hoynes, but even he can't defeat Mother Nature and her cold grasp.'

'We should say a few words to the Almighty,' said McKirdy. 'If this was happening at sea, we'd all be on oor knees in prayer. It's no different wae calamities on land, I'm thinking. I'm quite sure the dear Lord cares as much for those in peril in the woods as he does for those in a similar position on the waves . . . Though I know fine he's mair partial to seafarers,' he added to the general agreement of those gathered.

Solemnly, each man put down his dram and bowed his head in silent prayer for their missing companion.

Following a suitable period of silence, Andy Duncan spoke. 'It's the auld parable – *ninety and nine were safe in the fold, but one was lost in the hills* – or something o' that nature.'

'You're right, Andy,' said Munro. 'Though I canna just place what happened to the stray.'

There followed a heated discussion on biblical matters, which reached no conclusion other than no one could remember the fate of the lost sheep. McMichael had it roasted on a spit, until he was reminded that that was the fatted calf in an altogether different tale.

Hamish sat down heavily on an old chair. He remembered the time of his father's death, vividly remembering the feeling of utter despair, the ache in his heart that wouldn't go away.

Hamish reckoned that Hoynes was as close as any man could be to replacing his father, yet he felt nothing. Yes, he was worried for his skipper's wellbeing. But he had none of the gnawing sadness that had overwhelmed him before he knew his father was even ill. Hamish stood, and cleared his throat loudly, interrupting the ecumenical discussions taking place in the tiny bothy. 'He's fine, I just know he is,' he declared emphatically.

'This will be you at the second sight again?' said Peeny, an edge of sarcasm in his voice.

'It's just a notion – I have them from time to time.'

'Well, I hope it's better than your forecasting the day o' thon blizzards just before Christmas. As far as Sandy was concerned, all you predicted was a light flurry. It was the worst snow for twenty-odd years.'

'Sandy should have known better. The sight's no' designed for matters meteorological.' Hamish sighed and sat back in his chair, deep in thought.

Young Danny, feeling more empathy for his youthful colleague's plight than his elders, handed him a dram.

Hamish let the spirit warm him as he desperately hoped Sandy Hoynes would be the next to burst through the door.

24

Hoynes was chilled to the bone, miserable and – for maybe the first time in his life – losing all hope. He had wracked his brains to find a solution to his current predicament, but little had come to mind. He remembered a survival story from a book he'd read at school. The hero had found himself lost in the woods in freezing temperatures, just as he was now. But the construction of a turf shelter and the rubbing together of sticks to coax a fire into life, as good as it read on the page, seemed highly impractical when faced with the reality.

He could feel a terrible weariness settling in and recognised it for what it was. If he succumbed to sleep now, it would be a slumber from which he'd never wake.

Then, as he drew breath in through his nose one more time, he could smell it: the sea! And where the sea held dominion, no tree grew – or at least none he'd experienced in this part of the world. He would be free of the darkness, and by the light of the stars and the sickle moon make his way to safety. Hoynes forced his back off the tree trunk and sniffed at the air. The sea, he was certain, was to his left through the trees.

He moved from trunk to trunk, rough bark scraping his hands. He was aware that he was breathing heavily with excitement, so tried to measure it to slow down the thudding of his heart. The further he went, the less dark it became. Yes, he could see shadows now, the sharp outline of branches, the hulks of the trees themselves.

All of a sudden, the night opened out before him. Looking straight ahead, he took in the dark expanse of the sound, the twinkling stars above and the rippled shadow of a thin moon on the calm water.

Relief washed over him like a wave on a hot summer day. The fatigue disappeared in an instant, as, now free of the hampering pines, he took a great stride forward out of the forest's grip towards the element on which he'd spent most of his life.

But no ground met the sole of his boot. It was as though the world stopped for a moment. But that moment didn't last long. Hoynes felt the sickening pull of the abyss as he toppled forward into emptiness.

Cummings rushed into the cabin, concern etched across his face, a crew member behind him, bewildered. Marshall was curled up on one of the bench seats, screaming at the top of his voice.

'Sir! What on earth is the matter?' He placed his hand on Marshall's shoulder, but the collector brushed it away with such force that Cummings almost toppled over.

'Get away from me! Leave me alone – get back to your own world!' Marshall held his hands in front of his face like a boxer on the ropes, desperate to fend off blows from a superior opponent.

'Sir, it's me, Jocky Cummings. You must be having a nightmare.' As he said this, he was aware that crew member Jackson was gawping over his shoulder. He dismissed him without ceremony.

'What?' Marshall stared at Cummings as though he'd never seen him before, blinking in the dim light of the cabin.

'I think you've had a nightmare, sir. Nothing to worry about. We heard you screaming and feared the worst, but you're still hale and hearty.'

Marshall lifted himself off the bench and leaned against a table. He coughed and rubbed his eyes. 'Can't you smell it?'

'Smell what, sir?'

'The blood, man!' Marshall turned to face him angrily.

'There's no blood to be seen, sir. As I say, you've had a nightmare. Och, it sometimes takes a few moments to throw off the feeling. Just you sit down, and I'll get you some nice hot tea. That's bound to have you shipshape in no time.'

'Damn you and your tea and sympathy!'

'Sir?'

The look on Cummings's face was enough to bring Marshall back to something like himself. Though, in truth, he felt nothing like it. The vision of the ship and his encounter with the ghoulish apparition was all too fresh in his mind. He couldn't reconcile this experience with a dream – even a nightmare. It had all been so vivid – so real.

Marshall reached out and grabbed Cummings by the sleeve of his duffel coat. 'I'm . . . I'm sorry, Cummings. As you say, I must have drifted off and had a nightmare, eh?'

'Aye, that'll be right enough, Mr Marshall. No need to worry on my account. You sit back down. I'll have that tea with you in a jiffy.'

'Where are we?' Marshall sat back on the bench seat.

'As discussed, sir. We're not far from the Smuggler's Hole.'

'Where?'

'The place I reckon Hoynes might be hiding out. An old favourite of smugglers for hundreds of years, they say. Perfect. You can't see any boats berthed because of a big sandbar that obscures the bay. They say the Vikings built a settlement on the hill above. But I'm no' much for hill climbing, so I've never been there.'

'The Vikings, you say?' Marshall sounded suddenly anxious again.

'Aye, the very same. The Northmen settled most of Kintyre. A frightening bunch, they must have been.' Cummings immediately regretted what he'd said, as it seemed to have a most deleterious effect on the collector, who immediately held his head in his hands and groaned as though in pain. 'Sir?'

'Stay away from that bay, Cummings, do you hear me?' Marshall's voice was somehow both authoritative and uncertain at once.

'But we stand a good chance of catching Hoynes –'

'I don't care about Sandy Hoynes!' Marshall thumped the table with his fist. 'We anchor in the sound and make for Kinloch at first light.'

'I'm sorry, sir. I don't understand.'

'You don't need to understand, Cummings. Just do as you've been ordered!'

Cummings straightened up, bridling at Marshall's attitude. 'Very good, sir. We anchor off in the sound and make for Kinloch at dawn.' His voice was now clipped. The first mate turned on his heel and made to leave the cabin.

'Wait!' Marshall stopped him in his tracks.

'Yes, sir.' Cummings stood still, not turning to face his superior.

'I want to ask you something.'

'Go ahead, sir.'

'Have you ever heard of the Thin Places?'

Cummings turned slowly. Marshall was now looking at him with a pale and troubled expression. 'Indeed I have, sir.'

'What are they . . . it . . . whatever?'

'They are places where the past, present and future come close enough to touch, sir. Maybe even sometimes a bit more than that. Och, scientists and the like would have you believe that it's a lot of sheer nonsense. But I don't always hold with scientists. My guess is they'll soon work back to the way folk have thought for generations. There are many lives, many times – all within a whisper o' each other. It's what the auld folk here thought. Aye, and they knew mair than most, scientists or no scientists.'

'I see.'

'I'll away and get you that tea, sir.'

As Cummings made his way to the galley, he was sure that whatever Marshall wanted to call it, his experience hadn't been a nightmare. After all, in this place at this time of year, worlds came close. But, although he'd tried to make Marshall understand, it was a great leap of thought and reasoning for a man so steeped in logic and practicality. Still, that he'd had a taste of the Thin Places, Cummings was in no doubt.

25

Sandy Hoynes had always hidden a secret fear of falling. He supposed that, coming from a family that had spent so many generations at sea-level, it was natural to be mistrustful of heights. Yet, as these thoughts flashed through his mind, he could feel nothing beneath his feet but thin air.

He flailed desperately, trying to gain any purchase on shrub or rock to prevent his descent. He heard a roar – a cry of despair – and realised that the sound was coming from his own mouth. An image of his father, tall, strong and blond-headed. His mother's kind face smiling at him. The pet collie, Magnus, he'd had as a child, running towards him, big, wet tongue lolling. His life was passing before his eyes, just like the stories he'd heard of those nearing their end.

Time seemed to slow as he cast about wildly, trying to arrest his fall. Under the light of the stars, Hoynes saw his own arm arc above his head like the toppling of a steeple, and just as he felt his last hopes fade, he felt pressure on his right hand, then an iron grip. The next sensation was one of being pulled up, away from the abyss into which he was tumbling.

Before he knew it, Hoynes found himself lying on his back, choking and spluttering, trembling from head to toe in shock.

'You are a man who needs to be rescued often, I think.' The odd-sounding voice boomed above him.

Hoynes squinted into the darkness, still gasping for breath. 'I canna quite make you out, sir. But I'm right grateful to you. You wouldna happen to have some baccy on you, by any chance?'

A guffaw echoed above the crashing tide. The man – Hoynes's saviour – leaned down and looked him straight in the eye. 'I see you are no worse for your adventures.' The figure with the long, plaited blond hair and beard smiled. He was surrounded by a colourful glow that shimmered in the darkness like a guttering candle.

Hoynes gulped. Although the sight of the man who'd saved him brought fear to his heart, it was somehow comforting. 'It's yourself, Hona,' he replied, as though addressing one of his old cronies from the Kinloch fishing fleet.

'You remembered my name! This is very good. Though I wasn't sure I'd see you again so soon, I knew our paths were bound to cross. The connection we have is strong – even across so very many centuries.'

'I still canna understand. I know who you are – I read about you in a book from the library.' Hoynes realised how ridiculous this sounded as soon as he said it. Here he was – again – face to face with a man who died so, so long ago. But, that conundrum aside, Hona had saved his life – of that there could be no doubt.

Hona stood to his full height, towering over the recumbent Hoynes. 'I remember standing on this very spot when I saw the great silver bird in the sky.' He looked heavenward through the darkness, as though the image was above him. 'I knew it was not from my time. But then, I knew that time is nothing we can grasp or feel – it just is. It is all around us every day of our lives and beyond, yet can we hold it in our hands? No. I know in your heart that you, too, feel the pull of the Thin Places.'

Hoynes pushed himself up onto his feet. The shivering dread he'd experienced was gone now. Though the man before him was almost a foot taller than himself, he recognised the blue eyes that he'd noticed when the *Girl Maggie* was hopelessly lost in the blizzard only weeks before. 'There's so much I don't understand,' he said – meaning every word.

'It is not for us to understand, it is enough for us to be.' He looked around. 'Your little bothy is where my great hall once stood. Those nights, how I miss them.'

'So, where are you now?'

'I know not. I have passed into another realm and nothing remains the same, yet it is what is meant to be. We never disappear; our blood travels on. The blood in your veins is the same blood that is in mine. Always remember that, and never fear the end, for there is no end.'

Hoynes opened his mouth to speak, but already the image of the man clad in dark leather was fading. 'You don't hang about, eh?'

The shadow of his rescuer threw back his head and his laughter rang out once more, though it seemed more distant now, like an echo in a deep valley.

'I'm still no' sure where I'm going!' shouted Hoynes, suddenly realising that, despite his ghostly deliverance, he had no idea how to get back to the bothy. But the shadow had faded into nothing.

Hoynes stepped forward gingerly and inclined his head over the edge of the cliff. The drop was sheer and unforgiving. He swallowed hard and pictured his broken body lying on the jagged rocks far below. 'Aye, you're a lucky bugger, so you are, Sandy.' Though he wasn't sure if luck really covered what had just happened to him.

He looked left and right, puzzling on which way to go, in order to find his way back to the bothy. Behind him lay a thick pine forest.

Then, he heard the beat of wings. As he looked out over the sound, hovering in the air was a huge gull. It squawked loudly, regarding him with a beady eye, and then circled in the air, before flying straight ahead, a cry in its wake.

'Right. Good stuff. I know the score fae here. I'll just follow you.'

Being very careful where he trod, Hoynes skirted the clifftop, following the great seagull. Though it soared high above him, the bird was always close enough to see in the starlight. Its cry echoed again in the cold night air.

26

Back at the bothy, the mood was a sombre one, to say the least. Hamish had retreated to the darkest corner of the room, where he sat on the floor, hands clasped round his knees. He had neither a pipe of tobacco with which to ponder nor a glass of whisky to ease his sore heart. For there was no relief from the guilt he felt.

The older men in the party were sipping at their small glasses, huddled round the blazing fire. They knew that the revelry that had been planned was now at an end, for as soon as first light dawned, the search for Sandy Hoynes must commence.

'It's been a dark night indeed,' said old Andy Duncan, shaking his head. 'I wouldna be surprised if this is the last time anyone visits the stones to bring in the Auld New Year.'

'Why so?' asked young Danny.

'The whole experience will be forever tainted by the death o' Sandy Hoynes,' said McKirdy. 'What man could derive pleasure from this night in years to come? The thoughts will all turn to Hoynes. It'll put a right gunker on any celebration.'

'We don't know he's deid yet,' came a tremulous voice from the back of the room.

'This will be you with the sight again, eh, Hamish?' scoffed Peeny. 'As you'll hopefully come to understand with the passing years, practicality is what will keep you alive, no' some bloody nonsense that only exists in your own head.'

Hamish turned his face to the wall and said no more, though in his heart he could feel that his skipper wasn't dead. But there was no point arguing with such intransigent men as Peeny and McKirdy.

McMichael stared into the flames of the fire. '"Nearer My God To Thee", that was his favourite hymn.'

'Och no,' said Andy Duncan. 'When I was standing beside him at the Highland kirk at poor Tam Hastie's funeral he was fair belting out "Amazing Grace". Like an opera singer, he was. Well, maybe the odd waver on the higher notes noo and again, but the gusto was there, no doubt about it.'

'Nah. "Eternal Father Strong To Save," that's the one,' said McKirdy. 'No man o' the sea should be lowered doon to anything else; it stands to reason.'

'Aye, but the words are "for those in peril on the sea",' said Peeny. 'That hardly fits when you've frozen to death up in the woods, does it?'

'I've always liked "The Old Rugged Cross",' opined Malcolm Connelly. 'After all, he's likely perished on a hill far, far away.'

There seemed to be a general consensus around this choice being the most fitting. But the whole subject sickened Hamish to the stomach. 'That's it! I've had enough. I'll leave yous to get busy wae picking the floral arrangements and deciding on the purvey. I'm off to look for Sandy – dark or no dark.'

'Don't be a fool, Hamish,' said Andy Duncan. 'They trees are packed tighter than sardines. We'll be choosing hymns for you if you go out there.'

'Well, it's better than sitting here with a bunch o' auld ghouls. I'll take a stout lamp and plenty o' baccy – I'll be fine.' Then, in an afterthought: 'I'd be obliged if someone would lend me an extra coat, mind you. Two's better than one in this temperature.' Hamish jutted out his chin determinedly.

'I'll come with you,' said Danny, anxious to show some solidarity with his young companion. 'It'll be safer if one of us ends up in trouble.'

Peeny looked at McKirdy and shook his head. 'We canna let these boys go back oot in that cold alone.'

'You're right,' said McKirdy. 'Though it's a fool's errand, mark my words. Who's going to choose all our hymns? For the record, I'm in favour o' just a few sandwiches and tea. Man, you go to some funerals and it looks like a baking competition. Keep it simple, that's my motto.'

'Aye, and cheap,' said Malcolm Connelly. 'There's bound to be plenty pockets sewn into your shroud, and no mistake.'

'Well, I'm away, whatever yous think.' Hamish was searching about for another coat.

'Haud your horses, son,' said Andy Duncan. 'I'm too old for this caper, and so is Munro here. But if the rest o' you men feel that getting oot now to look for Hoynes is the right thing, then it must be done.'

'It's fine for you, Andy. Sitting beside the fire wae a dram when you know we're all risking oor lives,' said Peeny.

'If it was a man overboard in a heavy sea, you wouldna hesitate,' replied Duncan, nodding sagely.

This point was received with quiet agreement. While men of the sea would think nothing of mounting a rescue on their own element, the thought of heading into a dark, impenetrable forest was an alien concept.

'Let's get kitted out. Andy has the right o' it,' said McKirdy.

Slowly, reluctantly, the fishermen dragged themselves away from the warmth of the fireside and set to the task of filling oil lamps and shrugging on thick duffel coats and gloves. The odd glass of whisky was drained and the last puff of a pipe taken. But soon, with scarves wrapped around their faces, the attempted rescue of Sandy Hoynes was set to begin, regardless of how foolhardy the majority of those taking part thought the whole venture.

Munro and Duncan looked them up and down from their perch by the fireside.

'Aye, a right noble thing it is to see such brave men go about saving one of their own,' said Munro. 'I'll raise the Firdale men at first light, have no fear o' that.'

McKirdy swore under his breath as Hamish headed for the door. 'Here goes nothing,' he said to Peeny, who returned the sentiment with a raised eyebrow.

Hamish opened the door and took a step back, his mouth gaping open.

'What on earth is wrong wae him, noo?' said Andy Duncan, whose view of the doorway was obscured by well wrapped-up fishermen.

At that moment, a bulky figure with a blue face and frost encrusting his white beard staggered into the room.

'Sandy!' exclaimed Hamish, a broad smile on his face.

'Och, I knew he would be just fine,' said Andy Duncan levelly, taking a draw on his pipe.

'I take it there's a dram on the go?' said Hoynes through chattering teeth.

27

'I'm telling you, that's what happened,' said Hoynes, now sitting by the fireplace and wrapped up in numerous coats and scarves that made his already rotund figure look almost spherical.

'You're no' in your right mind wae the cold, Sandy,' remarked Andy Duncan. 'You take your time and sip at that hot toddy and get the warmth o' the fire. You'll soon regain your senses and wish you never came oot wae such nonsense.'

The old radio was crackling in the corner, though the music wasn't to the taste of most of those gathered, Danny having tuned it to Radio Luxembourg. To the strains of the Troggs' 'Wild Thing', Hoynes shook his head emphatically. 'Och, yous know nothing aboot it. One minute I was plunging to my death, the next I was dragged back to the land o' the living by something I'll never be able to explain.'

'I'm thinking you'll need to pay a visit to Doctor Fraser when we get back,' said Peeny. 'It might be the cold fair jumbling up your brain, but it could just as easily be the whisky.'

'What are you saying?' said Hoynes indignantly.

'We all like a wee goldie noo and again, Sandy. But you've developed a right habit o'er the last few years. We've a' noticed it.' Malcolm Connelly looked deadly serious.

'The cheek o' you! Man, it's only last year you got so drunk the polis had to take you hame. Aye, and you tried to evade justice by climbing up a lamppost on Long Road. Calling the constable every name under the sun, you were – aye, and some well beyond it, too.'

'My auntie had just died. It was all part o' the grieving process. That's what the GP said.'

'Oh aye. That could be a reasonable excuse, apart fae a couple o' wee issues,' said Hoynes. 'For one, your auntie died the year before, and you hadn't seen her since you were about three years old. Fair enough, it's bad luck to be trampled to death by a rogue herd of kangaroos, but the woman did move to Australia. She knew the risk. Spiders coming shooting oot o' the toilet when you're about your business. The place is fair stowed wae the deadliest o' beasts.'

Those gathered ruminated on this horror for a moment.

'Och, the whole tragedy o' it all just hit me that night.'

'Sure it did.' Hoynes took another sip of his toddy. 'But if every time a body who lost a relative in tragic circumstances took off up a lamppost, where would we be, eh? Man, the polis would have to be on it full-time. Criminals would be running amok.'

Andy Duncan piped up. 'I think it's fair to say, Malcolm, that the day you took to the drink was when big Campbell the lawyer telt you that instead o' the fortune you were hoping for in the poor woman's will, all you got was a painting o' Canberra and an ornamental boomerang. Is that no' right?'

Connelly looked mildly put-out by this. 'It was a bit o' a surprise, I'll admit. We'd all thought she'd done well for herself doon under. Though, I'd say the most disappointing aspect o' the whole thing was the only time I threw the bloody thing it near knocked Michael Kerr's heid off and flew oot over the loch. The bugger made no attempt to come back.'

This revelation was again met with a contemplative silence for a few moments.

McKirdy, being the diplomat he wasn't, decided to pour oil on troubled waters. 'Well, we all have problems in life. Sandy might think he's been rescued by Thor, and you've hellish problems wae boomerangs, but everyone is in one piece. We should be thankful.'

Both Hoynes and Connelly glared at McKirdy.

'Here, I'm no' so sure it's a "herd" o' kangaroos. That's surely reserved for coos, sheep and the like, is it no'?' said Hamish thoughtfully.

As a grey dawn broke over the sound, the Revenue cutter made for port at Kinloch in order to refuel.

Marshall, having spent much of what was left of the dark hours of night fretting in the cabin below decks, was now back on the bridge. Clean-shaven, straight and tall in his uniform, he was an altogether different specimen from the one who'd screamed and raved in his sleep only a few hours before.

'No' so bonnie today, sir,' said Cummings, manning the wheel as they sailed past the island and into the loch. The sky was heavy with cloud.

'Indeed not. We'll berth here until tomorrow – let the lads have some rest. It was a long night, Mr Cummings, was it not?'

'Aye, sir, it was that.' Cummings eyed his superior intently. 'And how are you feeling this morning, sir?'

'Never better. Tip-top, in fact.' He moved closer to his second-in-command. 'I trust we can keep my little nightmare between ourselves?'

'I've forgotten all about it already, sir.' Cummings looked straight ahead, his manner steadfast and reassuring. 'Mind, the lads could maybe do wae a bit R&R when we get to Kinloch, sir.'

'Yes, yes, of course.' Marshall coughed with embarrassment, realising that his odd behaviour had been witnessed by other members of the crew. He delved into his pocket and produced a wallet, from which he extracted a large, white five-pound note. 'They should be able to dine well on that, and enjoy a few libations into the bargain, eh, Jocky?'

'The very thing, right enough, sir. I'll make sure they know where it came from.'

'Excellent. Well, as soon as we tie up at the pier at Kinloch, I'll pay a visit to my old colleagues at Customs House. They tell me old McGregor is still in post, though he must be nearing retirement by now.'

'He is that, sir. A gentleman, too, I must say. Always a good bottle in his drawer, if you know what I mean?'

'Oh yes, that much I do remember.' Marshall nodded in agreement as they neared the twin piers at Kinloch.

28

It would be fair to say that those gathered in the bothy slept through much more of the morning than was their habit. But, being the fishermen they were, and despite some sore heads and dry mouths, by nine o'clock, one by one, they began to wake – apart from Andy Duncan who, the years and whisky having taken their toll, slumbered on, head tipped back and mouth gaping on his chair.

Hamish leaned across to Hoynes, who was drinking his habitual pint of morning coffee. 'Here, dae you think auld Andy is still in the land o' the living? He's no' moved for ages, and I canna even see any sign o' him breathing. I've been taking note this wee while.'

Hoynes, still wrapped up in several coats and a blanket, made his way between his companions, all in various stages of wakefulness, and stood over Andy Duncan. 'Man, it's hard to tell, right enough. What a tragedy that would be, eh? This trip has been ill-fated fae the start. The last thing we need is the auld fella hauling in his last net.'

Hamish and Hoynes's interest in Duncan prompted Peeny and McKirdy to sidle over to investigate.

'What's up?' said Peeny, stifling a yawn.

'It's Andy. He's no' moving. Aye, and I'm no' sure I like the colour o' him, neither. His face is as pale as the driven snow.'

'You're right,' said McKirdy. 'What a time this would be to lose a man like himself.'

Hoynes stroked his white beard for inspiration. 'This needs careful handling. Any sudden shock could be enough to stop his heart, a man o' his age.'

'You're right, Sandy,' said Peeny. 'You'll need to be right gentle, but we canna all stand here wondering if the poor bugger is deid or no.'

'You're no' often right, but you are on this occasion, Peeny. Leave this to me.' Hoynes leaned into Andy Duncan's ear, ready to whisper a gentle wake-up call.

'He's no' going to kiss him, is he?' whispered McKirdy.

Hoynes turned to face him, his expression showing little amusement. He quickly turned his attention back to Duncan, his mouth only an inch or so away from the older man's ear.

'Mind, he's quite deaf noo, Sandy. You'll need to give it a wee bit o' vent or we'll be none the wiser.'

This time, Hoynes decided not to turn round. He opened his mouth and was about to whisper into Andy Duncan's hairy left ear, when the old man's eyes shot open and he turned to face Hoynes with a blood-curdling scream.

Hoynes took two steps back, stumbling over Peeny and McKirdy's feet. 'Bugger me, Andy. You near gave me apoplexy!' Hoynes wiped his brow free of cold sweat with the back of his hand.

Duncan was breathing heavily, glaring at the figures standing over him. 'It's like a night oot wae the Munsters. What on earth were you trying to do, kill me? What poor soul wants to wake up wae your big coupon inches fae his face?

You look like Santa wae malicious intent.' Duncan held his hand to his chest as he tried to slow his breathing.

'Hang on, we might no' be out o' the woods yet,' said Peeny, taking in the pale-faced, gasping older man.

Duncan's reply was as unrestrained as it was curt.

Soon the company, amidst cups of tea and black coffee, were getting their kit together, ready to leave the Auld Stones for another year.

Young Danny was tasked with cleaning out the fireplace, while Hamish was set to work with a broom on the wooden floor. In no time at all, the bothy looked spick and span, and the weary mariners were ready to make their way back to the *Girl Maggie* and sail to Kinloch.

'That's a year we'll no' forget in a hurry,' said McKirdy as they made their way in single file down the steep path towards the Smuggler's Hole.

'Sandy won't forget it, anyway,' replied Peeny. 'Will you have us all rowing back hame? I know they Vikings liked a set of oars.' He winked at McKirdy.

Though Hoynes chose not to reply, he did address Hamish in quiet tones. 'Don't you be falling flat on your face like you did on the way here. This mob are on our tail wae their poor attempts at humour.'

They made their way along the sandbank and, with the rope ladder deployed over the side of the *Girl Maggie*, were all quickly aboard.

The grey water stirred as Hamish coaxed the engine into life, and Hoynes expertly steered his vessel out of the sheltered bay and into the sound.

✧

Marshall's visit to Kinloch's Customs House hadn't been the nostalgic return he'd hoped for. McGregor, the local officer and once his superior, was old and jaded, more than ready for retirement. Marshall could sense that his old mentor resented his visitor's rank, and the reception was polite but frosty. The 'good bottle' that Cummings had mentioned was not forthcoming.

'You were after Hoynes, I hear,' said McGregor, nursing a cup of tea.

'Well, we had information that proved to be inaccurate, to be exact.'

'Aye, I daresay. You have to be up early to catch the tide before Hoynes does. But, mind, he can be careless. When you keep getting away wae it, well, it makes you a bit complacent. Well worthwhile having a look at the boat before you go.'

'I've no idea when he'll be back. We're staying in port today. But duty calls, back in Glasgow.'

McGregor leaned back in his chair, looking across the green and the harbour beyond. 'I'd say that was the *Girl Maggie* at the pier now.'

Marshall bounced to his feet and rushed to the window. 'You're right! You'll have to excuse me. I want to have a little chat with Mr Hoynes.'

Without taking the time to look round the office where his career had begun, Marshall shot out of the room and quickly strode across the harbour green, the pier in his sights.

Their short journey had been uneventful and, with a fishing boat full of tired revellers, the banter conspicuous by its absence.

'No' so smart wae their tongues right noo,' said Hoynes from the wheelhouse to Hamish at his side. He was watching Peeny and McKirdy gather up their belongings, ready to disembark. 'It'll be dark early in their hooses, of that I'm sure.' Hoynes turned the wheel, coaxing his vessel next to the pier. 'You jump-to and tie her up, Hamish. I want to see if I can find my pipe.'

Hamish was over the side and securing a sturdy hawser round a bollard when he became aware of a pair of feet beside him.

'You – are you a member of the crew of this vessel?' The man in the distinctive Customs uniform addressed Hamish sharply.

'I am the first mate, sir. Can I help you at all?'

'You can indeed, young man. I want to have a look at your hold.'

Hamish felt a momentary twinge of terror quickly followed by relief at the thought of the cargo they'd carried away from Kinloch the previous day. 'I'll give the skipper a shout.'

'Never mind that. I don't need your skipper's permission to examine this vessel. Her Majesty's writ is long, you know. Please move aside while I board.'

Doing as he was told, Hamish stood back as Marshall deftly boarded the *Girl Maggie*.

The boat's passengers looked on with distaste as the collector hurried to the hold. Though he glanced at the wheelhouse, there was no sign of Sandy Hoynes.

By the time Hamish boarded the vessel and got to the wheelhouse, Marshall had opened the hatch and was making his way into the hold down a steep ladder.

'Sandy, the Revenue is aboard. He's away into the hold!' Hamish was breathless.

Hoynes shrugged his shoulders. 'If he's looking for fish, he'll no' find many.'

'It's no' fish he's after, skipper. You know fine what he'll want. We had a narrow escape last night – don't ask me how – but he's back on oor tail.'

'Good luck to the man. Now let me find my pipe!'

Hoynes's attitude calmed Hamish. But soon that calm turned into terror as Peeny called out from the prow, 'Sandy! Hamish! Your man's found something in the hold. He's examining it on the port side. Looks like a lemonade bottle.'

Hoynes shot up from the deck of the wheelhouse like a Jack-in-the-box. 'Make way, Hamish. This could mean trouble. It was dark when we were about oor business last night. I should have checked the hold for strays.'

A small crowd had gathered round Marshall as he examined the bottle under the grey sky.

'What's the meaning of this?' said Hoynes. 'You have no right to board a man's boat without the courtesy of informing the skipper.'

Without taking his eyes from the lemonade bottle full of whisky, Marshall replied, 'On the contrary, I have the right to do what I want.' He unscrewed the top of the bottle and sniffed at its contents. 'A good malt whisky, I'd say. The lab in Glasgow will confirm that, I'm sure. Any idea what it's doing in a lemonade bottle?'

By this time, Hoynes had made his way through the gathering and was standing next to the collector. 'Och, just an accident wae the proper bottle. I decanted it into that one. It's a sin to waste good whisky, so it is.'

For the first time, Marshall removed his gaze from the bottle and looked into Hoynes's face. He was about to open his mouth to speak when he caught sight of the skipper's piercing blue eyes. He tottered backwards. 'It can't be . . . no, it's not possible!' He backed away from Hoynes as though he'd set eyes on the Devil himself.

'The man's notorious, right enough. What have I been telling you all these years?' said Peeny. 'Aye, you've got to have some reputation to put the wind up a Revenue officer like that.'

'I can explain,' said Hoynes. He reached out for the bottle, but Marshall backed away.

'Leave me alone. I'll call the constable – I mean it!' There was a genuine look of panic in his eyes.

'Now, wait a minute. If you're no' careful, you'll . . .' It was too late. Marshall had retreated at such a rate that he collided with the port side of the *Girl Maggie*. He teetered for a while, desperately trying to regain his balance, but it was not to be. The collector fell backwards over the side, still clutching the lemonade bottle full of whisky.

29

Without a thought, Danny O'May dived over the side and, after a few seconds submerged under the cold oily waters of the loch, reappeared holding the collector by the collar of his sodden duffel coat. Peeny, just as quick to the task at hand, threw a lifebelt into the loch, while Hamish brought the rope ladder and extended it down the side of the *Girl Maggie*. He leaned over and, with the help of McMichael and a boathook, hauled both Marshall and O'May aboard.

Hoynes eyed the collector as various members of the party fussed over him. 'You seem to have lost your bottle, sir.'

Marshall looked back at him fearfully. 'Keep away from me!'

'Och, he's no' that bad – you get used to him,' said McKirdy.

'Can't you see his eyes, man – pure evil! I've seen those eyes before!'

'He can be a bit o' a scunner, I agree,' said Andy Duncan. 'But I wouldna go so far as to say he was evil.'

'The man's suffering from concussion,' said Hoynes. 'Hamish, you get over to the harbour master's office and phone an ambulance. A doctor is required, and no mistake.'

Making sure there were bodies between himself and Hoynes, Marshall began to wail. 'You've two hands!'

'Aye, I've always had the two hands, right enough,' Hoynes replied.

Marshall looked around the gathering. 'I want you all to see justice done here! That bottle must be retrieved, and this man must be brought to justice.'

'I'm thinking that won't stand up in court,' said Hoynes with a beatific smile. 'You'd have to dredge the loch. And in any case, there will be bottles o' all descriptions under there. You'll be hard pressed to identify the one you found on my vessel.'

The fishermen looked on as Marshall was stretchered into an ambulance, still raving and wailing in equal measure.

The excitement over, but not without reference to Hoynes's luck, the men who'd been to the Auld Stones drifted away, leaving only Hamish and Hoynes on the *Girl Maggie*.

'What on earth do you think was wrong with him?' said Hamish.

'Looked to me like one o' they nervous breakdowns. These high-flyers are prone tae such events, so I'm told. All that success goes to your head.'

'Aye, but we were lucky, eh?'

'Luck had nothing to do wae it. We were just bringing thirsty men a drink, as I've told you all along. Anyway, Hamish, you better get home. No doubt you'll have some free love to be at.'

Not willing to enter into another debate on the subject, Hamish made his way onto the pier and headed into town.

Hoynes, still determined to find his pipe, lit a match and knelt down on the wooden decking of the wheelhouse.

He cursed as, one by one, the matches burned down to his fingers and he had to light another one.

Just when he was down to his last match and about to give up, the flickering light caught something small and shiny.

'Aye, just the ticket. I knew I'd find it,' Hoynes said to himself.

But it was no briar pipe that Hoynes trawled from the deck. He stood up and examined the item. Nestled in his palm was the same brooch he'd seen at the Auld Stones. On that occasion it had burned his hand. This time, it was cool to the touch. He looked closer, admiring the swirling design of a longship with a snake's head, swirls and swords engraved expertly into the beautiful buttery gold.

'Thank you, Hona,' he said, grasping the small piece of jewellery in his meaty fist. 'I hope to see you again soon.'

From the leaden sky, a huge gull swooped over the *Girl Maggie* then circled back to head for the hills beyond, its cry echoing around the masts and hulls of the fishing boats nestling in Kinloch harbour.

Epilogue

1912

The boy panted as he tried to keep up with his father's long stride. The hill was steep, and the footholds that had been worn into it over the years were too far apart to be of use to his little legs.

Finally, his father stopped, held out a hand and pulled his son up the last part of the hill.

'That's us, son. Now follow me.' The man walked towards two small stones sitting in splendid isolation on the bare hillside.

'Is that the Auld Man and Woman, Father?' the little boy asked, his flaxen hair bright in the summer sun.

'Aye, there you are. This is them, right enough.'

Young Sandy Hoynes took in the objects with interest. 'They're no' very big, eh?'

'Don't worry aboot the size, son. Just you do what we said.'

Sandy thrust his hand into the pocket of his shorts and produced a silver pin.

'That's it, you know what to be at.'

The boy approached the stones and, in the one with the bowl-like depression, he carefully placed the pin.

'There, you see. You look after these stones, and they'll look after you. They've watched o'er oor family for generations – longer than anyone can remember. Aye, and mind how I showed you how to sail safely into the wee bay? It'll see you right one day.'

Young Sandy Hoynes smiled up at his father and followed his line of sight out across the sound. He felt warm inside, for there was something about this place that felt like home.